'I suspect that beneath your cool façade hidden fires burn,' Alex said.

'You—you shouldn't say such things. You seem to forget that you are my employer,' Cordelia retorted.

Alex sighed. 'Forget? How can I forget when you remind me of it whenever we find ourselves together?'

'I am sorry. I don't mean to. But it has to be this way. You do understand, don't you?'

'Do I have a choice? You are an extremely fascinating young woman. You intrigue me!'

Helen Dickson was born and still lives in South Yorkshire with her husband and two sons on a busy arable farm where she combines writing with keeping a chaotic farmhouse. An incurable romantic, she writes for pleasure, owing much of her inspiration to the beauty of the countryside. She enjoys reading and music; history has always captivated her, and she likes travel and visiting ancient buildings.

Recent titles by the same author:

THE RAINBOROUGH INHERITANCE
KATHERINE

LADY DECEIVER

Helen Dickson

First published in Great Britain 1997
Harlequin Mills & Boon Limited,
Eton House, 18–24 Paradise Road, Richmond, Surrey TW9 1SR

ISBN 0 263 80055 5

Set in 11 on 13 pt Linotron Times
04-9703-66642

Typeset in Great Britain by CentraCet, Cambridge
Printed and bound in Great Britain
by BPC Paperbacks Limited, Aylesbury

Chapter One

On the surface London was a town asleep, the sky several shades of grey above the soft orange glow from the street lamps. The streets were silent—apart from the occasional taxicab and the members of the smart set who careered recklessly about the empty streets in their fast open-topped motor cars, going from one night club to another or partaking in a treasure hunt, a new invention, dangerous and scandalous, but wildly exciting nevertheless.

The pavements were bereft of the seething mass of humanity which existed during the day, the new young set having taken to the fashionable night clubs and overcrowded cellars in the back streets of Soho and Leicester Square, where the syncopated rhythm of the jazz bands could be heard, and where people danced the night away to the Jog Trot and the Shimmy.

Triggered by the wastage and misery of the sombre years of the 1914–18 War, over now these past three years—the War to end all Wars, it was said—the sober, reserved English were letting themselves go in an abandoned form of escapism by casting aside the autocratic, stultifying ways which had existed before the War and replacing them with a new kind of permissiveness, creating a new society where the barriers of class and breeding were being swept aside.

Like the majority of this new, restless generation, Cordelia was wide awake as she drove her white, two-seater, open-topped Morris Oxford towards the flat she shared with her friend Kitty Wyatt in Bloomsbury—which, like her car, she had paid for out of a legacy left to her by her grandmother.

It had made her mother throw her hands up in horror, for she considered Bloomsbury a rundown quarter of London, full of seedy-looking houses and hotels. But to Cordelia and Kitty, who had given their flat their own originality and style, it was far grander than Cordelia's parents' town house in Belgravia.

Having recently completed a secretarial course at the Royal Holloway College for Women, in Surrey, Cordelia had been to a party in Holland Park, celebrating her success at passing her exams with friends. Sitting back on the leather upholstery, she delighted in the feel of the wind blowing through her short hair, breathing deeply of the crisp, scented, summer air, thankful that the rain which had been falling all day had finally ceased.

As she slowed down to turn off Oxford Street, from somewhere she heard the strains of a gramophone playing the popular song, 'I'm Always Chasing Rainbows', reminding her nostalgically of her home in Yorkshire, for it was a song her sister Emily had taken to singing on Cordelia's last visit there several weeks ago.

If, as the song suggested, she was chasing rainbows in her ambition to make her own way in life—for, since the end of the War, women had become more independent and enterprising—then she would be happy to go on chasing them. She was looking forward to seeing her family again, which was why she had left the party before anyone else in order to catch an early train up to Yorkshire.

Aware of a car coming up behind her, she glanced back, observing with some alarm that it was weaving about and full of boisterous revellers. When she saw it was about to pass her on the inside she swerved out into the road a little to let it pass, shaking her head in incredulity as it zoomed on ahead.

She didn't see the other car coming towards her, almost in the centre of the road, until it was too late. Frantically she swerved again to avoid a head-on collision, turning the steering wheel and applying the brakes, which caused her car to skid to one side on the wet road where it mounted the pavement before coming to a halt.

Angry and shaking, she climbed out to survey her precious car for damage, relieved to find there was none. Turning, she saw that the other car, a gleaming primrose yellow and black Daimler, having hit a lamp post, wasn't so lucky, for it had bent its running board as it had swerved to avoid the obstacle.

The driver, Captain Alexander Frankland—who preferred to be called Alex by his friends—immaculate in evening clothes, flung himself out. After surveying the damage to his car, he bore down on Cordelia like a tidal wave, his sleek, jet black hair, with just a hint of silver at the temples, gleaming in the light from the street lamps, and a murderous expression on his face. Looming over her, his mouth tightened and his eyes flashed dangerously as he glared down at her.

'What the hell did you think you were doing, careering round the corner in the middle of the road at that speed?' he demanded, with no hint of an apology, giving Cordelia no time to explain about the car full of young revellers she had swerved to avoid, who had merrily gone on their way with no notion of the furore their recklessness had caused. 'You could have killed someone.'

Cordelia stared at him incredulously, for she was convinced the accident was not entirely her fault. If this man had been on his own side of the road, she would have had no reason to swerve a second time.

'Me?' she gasped.

'Yes. Who else?'

'It was not entirely my fault,' she said, suddenly furious at having all the blame shoved onto her. 'I was forced to swerve a little in order to avoid a car that insisted on overtaking me on the inside. How was I to know you would be coming towards me driving down the middle of the road?'

Totally oblivious to the small crowd of curious onlookers that had appeared from nowhere despite the lateness of the hour, Alex stood with his hands on his hips, his grey eyes like ice set in a deeply tanned lean face with a strong determined jaw and his voice like steel.

'I might have known you would try and shelve the blame. I would expect nothing else from a woman driver. Although it's difficult to tell what sex women are these days,' he said, rudely looking her up and down, referring to her short-cut hair-style and slim, almost boyish figure dressed in a sheath of black sequins, bracelets and wrist chains encircling her wand-like arms and her long legs encased in flesh-coloured stockings. He had no intention of hiding the contempt he felt at finding a woman at the wheel.

Alex must have been aware of the storm that swept through Cordelia as she faced him, resolute, defiant, her small chin thrust forward. She favoured him with a glance of biting contempt.

'There is nothing wrong with my driving,' she said as calmly as she could. 'It's a pity the same cannot be said of yours. However, from what I can see, there is little damage done.'

'To your car, maybe, but the same cannot be said for mine.'

Cordelia cast a cursory glance at his car. 'It is only the running board that is a bit bent. It can easily be put right,' she said flippantly.

Alex's eyes narrowed as he tried to hold on to his temper. 'It may have escaped your notice, but that is a Daimler. Repairs do not come cheap.'

'Are you implying that I pay for the damage? If you are, then you can go and whistle for your money. I don't know who you are and, from what I have seen of you, I have no wish to know you—but you are quite the rudest man I have ever met. Dear me, if such a minor accident causes you to get so steamed up then I shudder to think how you would react to a major one.'

The anger provoked in Alex by what he considered to be Cordelia's reckless driving began to subside a little, and he felt a faint stirring of admiration for the way in which she faced him—self-assured and quite undaunted. Anger burned like a flame in her eyes and he was touched, despite himself, by her youth.

He took her to be one of the high-spirited

society girls who thought of little else but the frivolous pursuit of pleasure, whose life was one constant round of uninhibited fun and who thought it necessary to be a rebel, to outrageously defy the old order of society. No doubt she was off now to some wild party where she would dance until dawn to the new tunes which were sweeping across the Atlantic like a gale-force wind.

When he looked at her, there was no hint of the softening of his mood. His eyes, harsh and impenetrable, met hers, and, if she had but known it, they had once kept a regiment of soldiers in their place. But Cordelia, refusing to be intimidated by him, did not quail beneath them.

'No I am not implying that you should pay for it,' he said in answer to her question. 'I am well able to do that myself. But, tell me—just to satisfy my curiosity—does your family know you are careering about the streets unescorted at this late hour?' An odd quiver that might have been a smile passed over his lips.

'Not that it is any concern of yours,' Cordelia answered haughtily, 'but I am past the age of seeking my family's permission for what I do.'

'Then it is a pity they have allowed you to reach that age without teaching you to guard your tongue.'

Glancing around and realising that the people gathered round were listening to their harangue with open amusement, Cordelia pitched her voice lower when she next spoke, her expression resolute.

'If you must insult me, then at least have the courtesy not to do so in public. And it may have escaped your notice, sir, but since the War women have been liberated from the encumbrances of the past.'

Alex lifted one dark, contemptuous brow. 'No, it has not escaped my notice, and in my view it is certain to breed irresponsibility.'

'Then thank goodness few people share your view. If we choose to go *careering*, as you put it, about the streets alone, then we are entitled to do so.'

'At this late hour?'

'What are you saying? That women should not be out after dark?'

'Certainly not unescorted. It is dangerous—unless, of course, they want to be taken for a certain class of female,' he said with elaborate gravity. 'You do understand what I'm saying, don't you?'

Cordelia paled, unable to believe anyone could be so insufferably rude. 'I do and I do not care for it.' Abruptly she turned from him, opening the door of her car, eager to put an end to this unpleasant confrontation. 'I do not believe arguing like this will serve any purpose, so I will bid you good night,' she said tersely. 'And I hope that when you start up your precious Daimler it falls into a million pieces.'

It was only as he moved away that she became aware of two things about him—the first, that he was incredibly good-looking, and the second, that he walked with a slight limp. Suddenly, concerned that he might have been hurt in the accident, she was filled with self-reproach. Remembering her manners, which had temporarily flown out of the window at the thought of her precious car being damaged, she ran after him.

'Oh dear me,' she said, causing him to turn and look at her, surprised by her expression of concern. 'You're limping. You're hurt. I'm so sorry. I should have asked.'

Alex smiled, an absolutely chilling smile. 'No. You may rest easy,' he said, his voice as bland as butter. 'My limp was caused by a German bullet.'

A tide of hot colour stained Cordelia's cheeks. 'Oh—I am relieved to hear it,' but then her hand flew to her mouth when she realised what she had said. 'Oh—I—I didn't mean it to sound like that—that I am glad you were shot.'

He lifted one faintly ironic brow. 'No? Perhaps you were thinking that the German who fired it was way off target—that he should have aimed a trifle higher—at my heart, perhaps?'

'No—of course I wasn't,' she said indignantly. 'What I meant was—well—'

Alex sighed and his mood softened at her

apparent embarrassment. She was right, it was only a minor accident and nothing to get steamed up about, one that could easily be fixed—unlike other things in his life. Normally he would not have reacted quite so angrily, but he had been on edge before this young lady had caused him to swerve off the road, having spent an extremely tiresome evening dancing attendance on Diana Hibbert, the wilful, spoilt sister of his good friend James.

He had spent the past few weeks as James's guest at his chateau near Rouen, in France, and had intended spending the evening at his club with him in idle conversation. It had been unfortunate that Diana had come along. That she nurtured hopes of marriage between them was evident for she had hounded him ever since his wife had been killed in an air raid during the War.

But Diana would be disappointed; at the moment, he had no intention of marrying again. He had nothing but contempt for an institution that he had once believed would bring him fulfilment, but which had brought him nothing but misery instead. Once burnt, one learned to keep away from the flame.

Now he was strangely touched by this young woman's concern and he looked at her as if seeing her for the first time. She possessed the animal grace of a young thoroughbred, a femininity that touched a chord hidden deep inside him.

He looked at the short sleek cut of her honey-gold hair, which displayed to perfection the long slender column of her throat and the sharp, almost arrogant angle of her chin, which in turn was softened by the smoky hazel colour of her large eyes and the sensuous beauty of her face.

He suspected she was very much her own person—a woman of her time—but he would have been surprised to learn that she was also a woman who socialised with some of the best families in England. Entirely unexpectedly, his severity dissolved into a disarming smile.

'I know what you mean, miss—er—?'

'King.'

'Miss King—and it was remiss of me not to enquire as to whether or not you were hurt in the accident. I do apologise most sincerely. I am not usually so unmannerly and I realise I spoke to your most unfairly. Am I forgiven?'

Cordelia nodded, her lips curving in a smile. 'Yes. I suppose no one's perfect—least of all me. I was partly to blame for what happened so I apologise for any inconvenience I may have caused.'

'Then I forgive you,' he said gallantly, climbing into his car, but before he turned the key in the ignition to start the engine he looked up at her, his grey eyes twinkling mischievously and favouring her with a crooked smile, which rendered his face younger and less formidable. 'Providing, of course, my car does not fall into a million pieces when I start the engine. Goodbye, Miss King.'

Cordelia stepped back and watched as he started the engine and drove off down Oxford Street, wondering, as she drove the short distance to her flat—still feeling the intensity of his gaze, assessing and absorbing—who he was.

As Alex turned down park Lane, Cordelia would have been surprised to know that his thoughts still lingered on her. Miss King, she had said her name was. Funny how a name could stir up old, unwelcome memories.

Cordelia Hamilton-King was twenty-one, beautiful, headstrong and the youngest of the extremely wealthy Lord Langhorne's daughters. His estate was situated north-east of Leeds. Besides being the owner of 40,000 acres of land, and vast amounts of property in many of the northern towns, as a shrewd businessman he had increased his wealth by extracting rich deposits of coal from beneath his land.

He also had interests in steel mills in Sheffield, which had turned out munitions during the war, and textile mills in Manchester and Halifax, which had churned out uniforms for the soldiers in their thousands—all at an immense profit to himself.

The shortage of labour during the War, caused by the majority of young men joining the armed forces, had enabled women to go out to work to fill the positions left vacant. They had worked on the land, in factories, in the engineering shops; 100,000 had joined the auxiliary services to become nurses, and many more had entered government departments.

For the last year of the War, after returning from a six-month visit to America where she had been staying with friends, Cordelia's parents, after much persuasion, had allowed her to work and her father had secured her a position in one of the Government offices at Whitehall. It was there she had met Kitty, the daughter of Sir John Wyatt, an eminent politician connected to the Ministry of Defence.

Cordelia and Kitty had become firm friends from the start. Kitty was popular—her natural friendliness made it impossible for people not to like her. She was small, with a cat-like elegance, pale ivory skin and deep auburn hair which encapsulated her head in a riot of tiny, unruly curls.

There was nothing fussy about the flat the two girls now shared. The colour scheme of muted almond and green was restful to the eyes, the green hangings and upholstery blending tastefully with the furniture.

Wrapped in a peacock-blue silk dressing-gown, Kitty lay curled up on Cordelia's bed while she sat back against the pillows, sipping an early morning cup of tea which Kitty had brought her.

She had been woken to a barrage of excited

questions about the party of the previous evening, and responded by relating with patient detail and good humour who had been there and all that had taken place, because Kitty, much to her disappointment, had been unable to attend—the art gallery in which she worked had been putting on an exhibition, which had gone on until quite late.

In a moment of silence as Kitty digested the gossip, Cordelia looked across the room at the black sequinned dress she had worn, which was draped over a delicate, laquered Chinese screen in the corner. It brought back memories not of the party but of her encounter with the man in the Daimler. Her curiosity about him remained. Who was he? she wondered, letting her mind wander in idle speculation.

The fact that he drove a Daimler and that the cut of his suit had looked expensive and bespoke Savile Row told her he could be either a businessman or an aristocrat. He had a strong personality, reflected in his features, for she remembered his marked eyebrows and the strength in the arrogant line of his jaw. One thing she was certain of: he was a man of power and accustomed to obedience from others. If he had been an officer in one of the forces, this would explain it.

Her first impression of him had been that he was not a very pleasant character; now she was unable to work up any indignation at all for his initial angry behaviour when she remembered how charming he had been when he had apologised, the cruel line of his mouth softening with humour.

She sighed deeply, which brought Kitty's observant eyes upon her, frowning with careful scrutiny. Suddenly she sat up, smiling broadly, suspecting she knew the reason why Cordelia's attention seemed far away and why she had gone all dreamy-eyed.

'You met someone at the party last night, didn't you? Come on, Cordelia—tell me? Don't pretend you didn't. I know that look. You've gone all dewy-eyed. Don't tell me,' she gasped, 'Jeremy Bingham has finally plucked up the courage and asked you out?'

'No, of course he hasn't—and you know perfectly well I wouldn't accept if he had. Anyway—Jeremy wasn't at the party last night. He was playing polo somewhere or other and couldn't make it.'

Jeremy Bingham was a good-looking polo player to whom Kitty had introduced Cordelia at a garden party at Ranelagh the year before, when they had gone to watch the polo. The young man had been instantly attracted by her and was in the habit of seeking her out whenever possible. It was unfortunate for Jeremy that the attraction was not mutual. Cordelia had become quite fond of him as a friend and that was all.

'Then who was it?' persisted Kitty.

Seeing she was not to be put off, Cordelia placed her empty cup on the bedside table and looked at her. 'If you really want to know I did meet someone—but it's not what you think. I had an encounter on the way home with quite the most infuriating man I have ever met.'

'Oh. Not an admirer?' said Kitty, a trifle disappointed.

'Hardly. We were driving in opposite directions and somehow managed to run each other off the road.'

'Whose fault was it?'

'I think it was his fault—he said it was mine. He was the rudest, most arrogant man I have ever met—making some sarcastic remark about women drivers. I think he's of the opinion that women should still be chained to the house and their menfolk.'

'Ugh.' Kitty grimaced. 'How horrid. Were either of you hurt?'

'No.'

'Was there any damage to your car?'

'No—thank goodness.'

'What about his?'

'He hit a lamp-post which bent the running board. That was all. It was hardly worth getting all steamed up about—the way he did.'

'Why? What sort of car was it?'

'A spanking new yellow and black Daimler, which he clearly cossets as one would a child.'

'As you do yours,' Kitty replied with humorous sarcasm. 'Ever since you bought it you've been unable to think of little else. Still—there's little wonder he was angry if he drives a Daimler and it was damaged. He must be rich. I wonder who he was? What did he look like?'

'Oh, I don't know, Kitty,' Cordelia said with slight impatience, wishing she would change the subject. 'He was distinctly immemorable. And anyway, what difference does it make?'

'You never know,' she replied, rolling over onto her stomach and looking up at her friend mischievously, her eyes as round as an owl's in her exquisite face, 'you might meet him again some time.'

'That is highly unlikely.'

Kitty would not be satisfied until she knew all of it. Disregarding Cordelia's look of irritation, she continued to probe a bit further. 'How old did he look?'

Cordelia sighed with frustration. 'Thirty-two or three, I think.'

'Was he tall?'

'Yes—quite tall.'

'And good looking?'

'Yes—and he walked with a slight limp which he said he got fighting the Germans during the War. There—have I satisfied your curiosity about him—or do you wish to know whether or not he had one eye or two heads? If not, can we please talk of something else?'

Kitty's green eyes sparkled as she fixed her with an unblinking gaze, then gave a quaint pixie smile. 'Immemorable, you said. You don't fool me for one minute, Cordelia Hamilton-King. To say you were with him for so short a time, you certainly give a vivid description of him. He did attract you, didn't he? I can tell.'

Cordelia sighed, knowing she was beaten. Kitty was right. She did know her too well. 'Yes,' she confessed. 'I suppose he did. He was arrogant and rude—but he did apologise in the most charming way before he drove off.' She glanced at the clock on her dressing-table. 'Dear me,' she said, a note of urgency entering her voice. 'Look at the time. I'd better be getting ready. I do so want to catch the ten o'clock train up to Leeds. Be a love, Kitty, and do me some toast while I pack a few things.'

Clambering off the bed, Kitty scampered off into the kitchen to do her bidding. Swinging her long legs onto the carpet, Cordelia began opening drawers and throwing some clothes into a suitcase already open on the floor.

'When will you be back in London?' shouted Kitty over the noise of rattling crockery.

'That rather depends on what is happening at home. You know how much Mother hates me being in London. No doubt she's arranged lots of luncheon parties and dinner parties to keep me in

Yorkshire. She has a fit every time I mention getting a job. Oh, I know she accepted me working during the War, but when it ended she hoped things would go back to what they were like before. She approves of none of the decisions I've made about my future.'

'But she must have known, when you embarked on your secretarial course, what you intended?'

'I know, but she hoped that with time I might go off the idea and return home. She has never quite forgiven me for depriving her of the pleasure of my "coming out". She could not understand why I didn't want to be presented at Court and have a season like Georgina and Emily, but she gave up on the idea when she realised I would not be bullied into it.'

'Well, I suppose you can understand her, can't you? What with your brother David living in Leeds and Georgina away from home, and Emily soon to be married, it's only natural that she wants the best for you—to keep you close to her, especially since Billy...' Realising what she had said, Kitty fell silent, for whenever Billy's name was mentioned it evoked too many painful memories for Cordelia.

His name hung in the air. Cordelia paused as she was about to close the lid on her suitcase, her gaze coming to rest on the photograph of a fair-haired young man in military uniform on her dressing-table—Billy, her darling brother, three years older than she was. His real name was William, but everyone had called him Billy. He had meant the whole world to her. They had played together, grown up together—until the War had come. When he was old enough, he had joined up.

Like thousands of other young men, Billy hadn't come back. Cordelia had been in America when the news had reached her and she had gone home immediately to Edenthorpe to be with her family. She didn't know the details of his death. It was enough for her to know he would never come back. Her parents had been devastated, finding it difficult to speak of him. It was her brother David, an officer in the army, home on leave, who had told her that Billy had been killed at the third battle of Ypres.

Coming to stand in the doorway, Kitty looked full of remorse. 'Oh, Cordelia, I'm sorry. I spoke without thinking—which is all I ever seem to do. I don't know why you put up with me—truly I don't.'

Cordelia banged the lid down on her suitcase with a determined thud and smiled at her fondly. 'Why should you be sorry? I don't mind talking about Billy. He was my brother, after all. At home no one ever speaks of him. It would be much better if they did—it's just as though he never existed. And,' she said, going over to her and giving her an affectionate hug, 'I put up with you because you are my best friend. What would I do without you?'

Somewhat mollified Kitty grinned, and at the smell of burning toast scampered back into the kitchen. 'By the way,' she called, scraping the burnt bits into the sink, 'you will be back for Ascot in two weeks, won't you? I'm relying on you to help me pick some winners. You know how hopeless I am.'

'I'm just as hopeless as you—but of course I'll be back. As if I'd miss the high point of the season,' Cordelia replied. Ascot was an event she always looked forward to.

Chapter Two

Cordelia had been correct when she had told Kitty that her mother would have arranged plenty of social events to keep her occupied at Edenthorpe. If she had expected a few quiet days alone with her family, then she was disappointed. Her mother was a tall, stately woman with an inbred upper-class instinct for doing the right thing.

The passing of the War had touched her, as it had almost every other family in the land. The loss of her son, Billy, and her son-in-law—leaving her daughter, Georgina, a widow with two young children—had sadly disillusioned her. The feeling of security that had once existed was gone and the old glamour and courtesies of the world in which she had been reared were receding into an age gone by; the only way she knew of holding onto the past was by keeping to the old traditions.

She no longer visited London, which Cordelia

considered strange; before the War, when her father had been absorbed in his favourite pastimes of hunting or shooting, she had often stayed for lengthy periods at their house in Belgravia, with herself, Emily or Georgina—or all three of them—socialising on a grand scale, shopping or visiting the theatre. The house was now up for sale; no one stayed there any more. It was as if the world that existed outside Edenthorpe had become shadowy and unreal for her mother.

Cordelia noticed how the numbers of friends and acquaintances had increased at Edenthorpe; her mother seemed indefatigable in her efforts to entertain. She threw endless cocktail and dinner parties, with a queenly generosity, at which she always excelled and which were always lively—the conversation animated, the food excellent and the wines of the finest quality.

Sometimes the guests played billiards or bridge after dinner or, during the summer months, spilled out onto the velvety sloping green lawns which surrounded the house.

Cordelia loved Edenthorpe, standing against a backdrop of fields and moorland. It had been in the family since the Middle Ages and each generation had added bits and pieces to it. The expenditure of such a great house was a formidable sum to Lord Langhorne, even with the substantial income he received from his mills and coal mines.

Cordelia spent her days in languid contentment,

taking part in the nonsensical gossip with the guests her mother had invited to her luncheon and picnic parties, playing tennis, swimming in the river with Emily or lounging on the grassy banks watching David fishing.

He was the oldest of Lord Langhorne's children who, already immersed in the family business, would one day inherit the wonderful green acres of Edenthorpe. He had travelled from Leeds for the weekend and Georgina, bereft without her husband, had come from her home in Knaresborough with her two children.

It was good for them all to be together as a family again, but it was at these times that Billy's absence was more pronounced. Cordelia experienced a strange perception of unease whenever she mentioned him; he was a subject everyone seemed careful to avoid.

A pained expression would always appear on her mother's face and she would turn away, careful to conceal the real depth of her loss. Cordelia was distressed by this; she felt sure everyone would feel better if they could bring themselves to talk about him. It was as if he had never existed.

The subject of Cordelia's future was raised when they were gathered around the dining-table one evening. David had returned to Leeds and Georgina and the children had gone back to their home in Knaresborough. Cordelia had been regaling Emily with tales of what life was like in London, what tunes were being danced to and the latest fashions.

Her sister was eager to know all about the clothes, for she made no secret of her admiration for Cordelia's fashionable new jumper suits designed by Chanel, which everyone was beginning to wear, and the clinging crêpe-de-Chine skirts, so different to the cumbersome, heavy long skirts and tailored coats of her mother's era that Emily still wore.

Certain that this kind of gossip would have a disruptive influence on Emily, who hung wide-eyed onto her younger sister's every word, her mother cast her a disapproving glance. All this talk of independence and liberation was, to her, anathema in an alien world. Cordelia sighed, understanding why her mother wished to live within the old order of things, but wishing she would try to accept the changes that had been brought about by the War.

'Times have changed, Mother. Nothing is the same as it was,' she said kindly.

'I still think young people should be subjected to more discipline. Young ladies in particular are inclined to too much frivolity these days. What do you intend doing now you have finished your secretarial course, Cordelia?'

'Getting a job, of course. That was the whole point of doing it.'

A look of despair entered her mother's eyes. 'You know how much I am against that. I did so want you to be presented at Court like your sisters. You were always such a bright, popular child. I had hoped you would be married by now—with children.'

'Then I am sorry to disappoint you, Mother,' said Cordelia with patience, exchanging a furtive, knowing glance with Emily, who was seated quietly across the table, content, as was her nature, to eat her food and to remain silent and let the conversation take its course.

'I am no longer the bright, carefree young girl of before the War,' Cordelia continued, 'who had no thought beyond doing all the things her sisters were doing—coming out—dancing and parties—marrying some dashing, good-looking young man who would whisk her away to his castle in the clouds. She disappeared somewhere along the path to womanhood,' she said with an underlying bitterness when she remembered Billy, his life cut short by a German bullet.

'What choice did I have? I was too young to be presented at Court before the War; when it started, no one believed it would drag on so. And now, for me, like so many other people, the War has changed everything. I no longer want all that.'

Lord Langhorne, a tolerant man who was content to let his wife have her own way in most things, and expected little of his children except that they conduct themselves in the well-behaved, proper manner in which they had been brought up to become responsible adults, sensed a storm brewing, which always seemed to be the case these days when Cordelia was at home and the subject of her future was raised.

In an attempt to avoid such an unpleasant situation developing, he shifted his gaze from the straight-backed figure of his wife to the tense, beautiful face of his youngest daughter, unable to resist the tide of love and admiration that swept over him when his eyes met hers.

She was in possession of an independence of mind and spirit and a natural confidence that was lacking in her older sisters. He was filled with admiration for her decision to stand on her own feet and had often thought it a pity she had not been born of the male gender, for she would have been a tremendous asset to Edenthorpe and the business.

'Do you have a young man in London, Cordelia?' he asked calmly.

'No, Father. No one special, that is.'

'Then that is a pity,' persisted her mother. 'Georgina did well for herself and so has Emily. She is to marry an extremely personable young man.'

Cordelia again looked at her mother. 'And so will I do well for myself, Mother, but not by marrying—at least, not yet. Besides, all the young men of my generation were decimated by the War—and most of them who came back are crippled and maimed in some way.'

'Sadly that is so,' conceded her mother with a deep sigh. 'A high proportion of those killed and wounded were officers belonging to the peerage, who, like David, received their commissions on the strength of certificates granted by the universities.'

'Which was also the case with Billy,' said Cordelia quietly, deeply saddened that he was always omitted from the conversation.

'Yes,' said her mother quietly, her eyes becoming glazed. 'As was the case with Billy. But David was not the only one to come out of the War unscathed. Several of our acquaintances have sons who came back.'

Knowing what her mother was getting at and suddenly having no appetite for her food, Cordelia put down her knife and fork and folded her napkin, placing it beside her plate.

'I'm sure that is so, Mother,' she said, picking up her glass and taking a sip of wine with the perfect composure of a lady, 'but I cannot see any eligible young man beating a path to my door—and I sincerely hope not.'

'Now you have finished your secretarial course, what field of work do you intend entering?' asked her father.

Cordelia shot him a grateful look, knowing he

had deliberately asked the question in order to steer the conversation away from the subject of marriage. She was glad that, unlike her mother, he did not disapprove of her decision not to follow in her sisters' footsteps, that he sanctioned her intentions.

'I'm not sure yet. I'd like to gain some experience first. I may take something temporary while I get the feel of things.'

'Would you not consider joining the family business?' he offered. 'There is always room for you with David in Leeds. I know he'd be more than happy to have you along—show you the ropes, so to speak.'

'No, Father, thank you,' she said, a positive, determined light burning in her eyes. 'I intend to get ahead on my own merit. The only drawback to that, however, is that to be a Hamilton-King—to belong to a well-known family—will be fatal to my career. Employers will either embrace or reject me because of who I am. I don't want that.'

'What are you saying?' asked her mother.

'I've decided to shorten my Christian name to Delia and dispense with Hamilton from my surname and simply call myself King. Delia King sounds less snobbish that Cordelia Hamilton-King, don't you think?'

Her mother looked more than a little appalled, shocked and bewildered. 'Why—all this is very irregular, Cordelia. I've never heard of such a thing.'

'Perhaps not, but Cordelia is right,' said her father, firmly in support of his daughter's decision. 'If she wants to become successful, then it is essential that she takes on her own identity. The name "Hamilton-King" is too well known—especially in the business world. It could prove to be a burden—an embarrassment, even though I do say so myself—to her future success.'

Cordelia beamed at him. 'Thank you, Father. I knew you'd understand.'

As promised Cordelia was back in London for Royal Ascot, a colourful and fashionable highlight of the social season. They were to be escorted by Jeremy Bingham and his good friend Alfred, a fellow polo player in whose car they were to travel the twenty-six miles to the famous racecourse in Berkshire for Ladies Day, the highlight of which, and the most prestigious race of all, being the Ascot Gold Cup.

Jeremy was over the moon because Cordelia had agreed to let him escort her, but she had made it quite plain that, fond though she was of him as a friend, that's all it was. Her career was too important to her at this point in time to become entangled with anyone emotionally. With that he had to be content.

All were in high spirits—Cordelia more so than

the others, for when she had returned to London from Edenthorpe it was to find a letter waiting for her. On reading it, she learned she had been successful in obtaining an interview for a position she had applied for in Norfolk, which she had seen in the situations vacant column in *The Times*. She was to travel to Norfolk the following week.

Kitty had agonised over which outfit to wear for days, for race frocks were the pivot round which all dress schemes evolved. She finally settled on a black mousseline gown and black picture hat with a black ostrich plume, while Cordelia wore a dress of cream lace over satin with a blue swathed sash and a cream lace wide-brimmed hat with cerise velvet streamers.

When they were going out to the car, Cordelia cast a look of doubt at Kitty's choice of dress.

'What's the matter?' said Kitty, noticing. 'Don't you like it?'

'Yes—but black? Is that wise?'

'I think so. Nothing is as effective in a crowd of colour as a black dress. You'll see,' she said with confidence, climbing into the car and shuffling along the leather seat in order to make room for Cordelia. 'It will make everyone else's gown seem tawdry in comparison.'

Cordelia was doubtful about that, but said nothing as she climbed into the back seat alongside her in Alfred's open-topped tourer. It was to turn out that Kitty's inspiration was an inspiration shared by many other ladies at Ascot that day—even a few in the Royal Enclosure—and some with white as a contrasting colour, producing a positively magpie appearance.

The day promised to be hot—in fact, it turned out to be one of the hottest at Royal Ascot within memory. They both took parasols to protect their delicate complexions from the enquiring rays of the sun, leaving their wraps and coats in the car when they arrived at the racecourse, where a holiday atmosphere already prevailed. The crowds were huge, but not quite as large as they had been on the first day, which always drew a large gathering.

From the stands they watched the King and Queen, with other members of the Royal Family, drive up the course in open landaus in Ascot state amid hearty cheers from the crowd. But, despite the presence of the Royal Family, Ascot was by no means a stuffy affair.

The highlight of the day was the Gold Cup, run over two and a half miles. It was the best of the races staged during the four-day June festival, its long history having produced some thrilling and close finishes but, before that, there were two races to get through.

Alfred and Jeremy, already overheated in their morning coats and top hats, went off to one of the marquees in search of liquid refreshment, while Cordelia—who had already avidly studied the races and the form of the horses in the *Sporting Life*—and Kitty, clutching their race cards, went to the paddock to see the horses for the first race being paraded in the ring. The sun had scorched the grass of the enclosure and paddock dry.

People jostled with each other for a better view of the horses, conversation being about what would win, the usual laments on the no-hopers and criticisms over other people's clothes. Finally, both choosing a horse called Monarch, they went to place their bets.

Cordelia had a good knowledge and instinct for horses, choosing the horse as Billy and her father had taught her—after assessing its form and time ratings—whereas Kitty chose it because she liked the name and because it seemed appropriate with the monarch, King George V, being present. Jeremy and Alfred preferred last year's winner, Diadem.

For a while Monarch was invisible, tucked away behind with Diadem in the lead, but he came on to challenge and Cordelia and Kitty watched and shouted in jubilation as he tore past the winning post. Jumping up and down, they embraced ecstatically.

'Bravo!' shouted Kitty. 'I knew Monarch would win. Let's go and celebrate over a glass of champagne, shall we?'

'Good idea,' beamed Jeremy, tearing up his useless betting ticket and throwing the bits over his shoulder. 'And I hope the drinks will be on you, girls.'

Laughing, Kitty poked him playfully in the ribs with the point of her parasol then left with Cordelia to collect their winnings.

The day had got off to a good start, or so they thought; at that moment a primrose yellow and black Daimler had just turned in through the gates of one of the car-parks, an irate Alex Frankland at the wheel. He had come with his friend James Hibbert, a racehorse owner passionately involved with the game.

James had almost begged him to escort his sister Diana to Ascot. Alex would have preferred not to, but considered it would be bad manners to refuse after James had played such a generous host when he had stayed at his chateau, so he had agreed.

Alex had not been to Royal Ascot since before the War. It was a meeting he had always liked, his interest in the horses rather than the people who watched. He liked the fiercely competitive nature of racing at Ascot and the tricky, demanding conformation of the course which conspired to cause many an upset in form.

Having offered to drive James and Diana he had allowed ample time, but Diana had decided to change her outfit at the last minute, resulting in a late start. Alex was annoyed; after what he considered to be an unnecessary delay, they had been held up in traffic on the way to the course. They had progressed at the rate of one mile in a good deal over an hour, the heat getting worse by the minute. When they arrived, it was to find they had missed the first race.

'I'm off to get a drink,' said James. 'I'm raging with thirst, old boy. Join me?'

Alex glanced at his watch. 'No. It's almost time for the Granville Stakes. I'm going to take a look at the horses in the paddock. I see they're already parading.'

'I'll go with James and join you later,' said Diana, following her brother towards the Members' enclosure.

Making his way towards the parade ring, Alex pushed his way through a sea of brightly tinted sunshades towards the front to see the thoroughbreds on parade, feeling a surge of admiration, as he always did, when he gazed on such magnificent horse flesh.

When he returned to his home to take up civilian life—once the house was restored after having been used as a convalescent hospital for soldiers wounded during the War—he was determined to fill his stables, as they had been before the war, with horses just such as these.

Alex looked casually among the crowd gathered around the ring to see if there were any familiar faces. His eyes came to rest on a tall, slender young woman dressed in cream lace across the ring from where he stood.

She had her head bent as she studied her race card and was clearly a keen racing enthusiast for she had the *Sporting Life* tucked beneath her arm. He could not see her face because of the wide brim of her hat. Just as he was about to shift his gaze to the jockeys, each in the owner's colours, who were beginning to mount, she lifted her head, uncertainty on her face, clearly undecided as to which horse to put her money on.

He recognised her immediately as the young woman who had accused him of running her off the road in her motor car. Remembering the deep impression she had made on him then, interest flickered deep inside him and a slow smile curved his lips as he continued to watch her.

Over at the other side of the ring Kitty had noticed the way that Alex was staring at Cordelia and, nudging her, she said, 'Don't look now, Cordelia, but there's a gentleman at the other side of the ring looking at you as if you're fit to eat. I don't know whether or not you know him, but he seems more interested in you than he does the horses.'

Slowly Cordelia dared to look across the crowded ring. There were so many people it was difficult to know where to look at first, but then she saw him, her eyes drawn to his like a magnet. He was tall and incredibly distinguished-looking in his black morning coat and silk top hat. Recognition made her eyes open wide and she could do nothing but stare.

'Who is he?' asked Kitty impatiently.

'Do you remember the man I told you about—the one who ran me off the road on the night of the party? Well—that's him.'

'Gosh! He's gorgeous. I wish a man would look at me like that. It's obvious he remembers you.'

A woman suddenly appeared at his side, tall and beautiful and with full scarlet lips. Her gown was of seagull-grey silk belted with jade-green velvet, her large black hat covering her sleek hair of the same colour, curled feather fronds sweeping from left to right lying in the brim. She followed Alex's gaze, curious as to what could be holding his attention so intently.

On seeing Cordelia, her eyes narrowed and she placed her gloved hand possessively on his arm, whispering something in his ear and drawing him away. Cordelia, wondering who he could be, watched them turn and become swallowed up in the crowd.

Her reverie was interrupted when Kitty and their escorts began discussing which horse to back.

'Oh—I don't know,' said Kitty in a quandary. 'Sunblaze or Black Gown. What do you think, Cordelia?'

'Well, Kitty,' she answered, trying to put the gentleman who had disappeared from sight to the back of her mind, 'Sunblaze is short priced, which shows he is much favoured—but I think I'll stick with my first choice—Black Gown—if he can be persuaded to start.

'And if you're undecided,' she laughed, 'as with Monarch in the last race, which you chose because you liked the name and thought it was a good omen with the King being present—then your own black gown might prove to be just as lucky.'

With that it was decided and they left the paddock to place their bets. Once again their luck was in; once Black Gown got off from the start, he was hard to beat.

After gulping down glasses of champagne, they returned to the paddock where Gold Cup excitement was beginning to build up. Having already made up her mind days ago which horse to back, Cordelia left the other three still undecided and went to look at the betting to see where she could get the best price.

Suddenly, aware of someone coming to stand beside her, she turned, finding herself looking up into a pair of quizzical grey eyes. Totally unprepared for the effect his presence had on her, her stomach lurched and her eyes opened wide with surprise.

'So—it *is* you,' Alex said, his voice rich and deep. 'I thought I recognised you. I am glad to know my memory of the occasion of our previous encounter is not at fault—and,' he went on, his eyes narrowing and his smile deliberately meaningful, 'I was also pleased to see you had not forgotten me either.'

Hot colour washed over Cordelia. 'No,' she replied sharply, irritated by the way he said it, as if she had thought about nothing else but him since that night. 'I do remember you. Your car is repaired, I hope?'

'Yes. Like new.'

'Then I am happy to hear it. You will have to be more careful in the future.'

'Oh—I am,' he laughed. 'I take great care in keeping out of the way whenever I see a young lady behind the wheel of a motor car.'

Unsmiling Cordelia looked up into his laughing grey eyes. 'Why—how very considerate of you,' she said with a hint of sarcasm, 'for little do they know they are in danger of being run off the road.'

Alex bent his head slightly in acknowledgement that her remark had hit home. 'Touché,' he smiled, feeling a stir of admiration for her quick repartee.

'Are you enjoying the day?' Cordelia asked politely, turning her attention back to the line of bookmakers with the crowds milling around them to see who offered the best price for the Gold Cup.

'Unfortunately, we missed the first race because of the traffic. Considering there is an air ship that has been manoeuvring over the suburbs of West

London for the greater part of the day, working in conjunction with the police on the ground, supposing to superintend the traffic on the roads leading to Ascot, it did little to alleviate the congestion. And yourself? Are you enjoying Ladies Day?'

'Yes—thank you.'

His eyes swept over her carefully chosen apparel appraisingly. 'I must compliment you on your dress. You look charming.'

'Thank you,' she said somewhat drily, wondering how many ladies here today he had said the selfsame thing to. 'I am flattered.'

'I see you have the *Sporting Life* to hand. Are you having any luck with the horses?'

'Yes. So far I've managed to pick the winners of the last two races.'

Impressed, he nodded slowly. 'You like horses?'

'Very much.'

'So—tell me, what are you going to reinvest your winnings on for the Gold Cup? With luck like yours I might be tempted to follow suit.'

'I think my luck is beginning to run out,' she said tartly, with slight reference to his presence, but if he had noticed it, then he gave no indication. 'But, since you ask, Periosteum is my choice.'

Alex glanced down at his race card with a doubtful frown. 'Is he? I think he's altogether lacking in class for a Gold Cup candidate. I myself fancy Silvern or Juveigneur. Both have had good races.'

'I agree. Silvern has been making improvement and he'll like the hard going. He's a favourite, I know, and he seems to be gaining most admiration in the parade ring, but I doubt his ability to stay the course.'

Alex frowned in disagreement. 'He showed up well at Newmarket when he ran with four other probable entries featured in the Cup today.'

Without being aware of it, Cordelia discussed the race with animation, her hazel eyes shining with interest. 'Yes, but the distance then was a mile shorter than it is here today.'

'And Juveigneur? What is your opinion regarding him?'

'He's a much better-looking animal than he was last year and is by no means to be disregarded. He might run into a place but I think Periosteum may beat him.'

Alex nodded, regarding her closely. 'You are extremely knowledgeable, Miss King.'

Cordelia looked at him with some degree of surprise that he should remember her name. 'Oh! You remember my name.'

'Of course. How could I forget after such a memorable encounter? You appear to be a real racing enthusiast.'

'Not really—although I know the life. My father and brothers taught me.' She wondered what he would say if she told him that her father had a string of racehorses and usually would have had one or two at the Ascot meeting but, owing to the miners' strike and the terrible depression which hung over the country, he had more important matters to occupy his mind at Edenthorpe.

'It is clear you like horses.'

'Yes. The thoroughbreds here at Ascot are quite spectacular.'

'The privilege lies in being fortunate to see them race, don't you think?'

The harsh lines of his face had dissolved into an unexpectedly charming smile and his gaze rested on Cordelia's upturned face warmly. Suddenly she felt ill at ease, not knowing what to say. His look was penetrating, as if he wanted to look right inside her mind.

She found him fascinating and, moved by his close proximity, was tempted to ask his name but resisted the impulse on instinct—even though her heart cried out to know. He was a man fully in possession of himself and she sensed it would be dangerous to get to know him. To let her emotions become involved with a man with such a powerful personality could destroy her peace of mind.

At that moment the woman she had seen him with in the paddock appeared by his side, her eyes sliding insolently over Cordelia, who stepped back quickly.

'Please excuse me,' she said. 'I must go. My friends will be wondering where I've disappeared to.' Without further ado she vanished into the crowd.

Chapter Three

After an afternoon of overindulgence, with lobster and salmon washed down with sparkling champagne, spent bemoaning his bad luck over his failure to back a winner earlier in the day, Jeremy's luck suddenly changed in the final two races when his horses romped home. Jeremy and Kitty were celebrating their success, each getting sillier and sillier. Alfred, having the unenviable task of driving them all back to London, had consumed little in the way of alcohol, and neither had Cordelia.

She was content to sit in the sun and watch, smiling indulgently at Kitty and Jeremy's high-spirited antics. She lazily thought, when Jeremy disappeared inside the marquee to fetch another bottle of champagne, that being the eldest son of a lord, and with his sleek blond locks and the lithe, athletic body of a polo player, he had the kind of pedigree her mother would approve of, that she would be more than happy if Cordelia were to take him back to Edenthorpe.

Several young people clustered around the marquee shared the same kind of abandoned exuberance. Jeremy returned with a fresh bottle of champagne, his fingers placed over the uncorked neck as he proceeded to shake it vigorously. Kitty collapsed onto the grass in a fit of uncontrollable giggles while everyone else whooped with laughter and moved out of range of the expected shower of champagne.

When he released his finger, after a final vigorous shake, sending a fizzing, frothy fountain out in front of him, unfortunately, at that moment people were beginning to leave the Tattersall's and Member's enclosure to make their way back to their cars, and two of them were the recipients of Jeremy's spurting champagne.

Behind the stream of liquid, buoyed up by the excitement of the moment and unable to focus properly, Jeremy had no notion of the havoc he had caused. Cordelia, who had been laughing at his harmless antics, suddenly stopped, the smile becoming frozen on her lips. The laughter from everyone turned to gasps.

The woman who had taken the full blast of the champagne was absolutely livid, her face as white as paper. She looked down at her dress in horror, the seagull-grey silk creation soaked and clinging to her body like a second skin, outlining all the contours beneath it.

There was a complete hush as everyone exchanged uneasy glances. Observing the ruin to Diana's dress, Alex stood beside her with a dangerous calm. His eyes swept over the high-spirited group frozen into immobility, with varying degrees of criticism; of them all he singled out Cordelia, his expression hard enough to make hell freeze over.

Fully aware of the catastrophe he had caused, Jeremy went puce with horror, quickly stepping forward to apologise.

'I say, I'm most awfully sorry,' he said, taking his handkerchief from his pocket and offering it to the lady in an awkward gesture to mop up some of the liquid. 'I didn't see you.'

Angrily the woman knocked his hand away. 'That was obvious,' she flared. 'You fool. How dare you? Look at my dress. It's totally ruined and I have to travel all the way back to London.'

'Well—you'll soon dry in this heat,' said Jeremy, which did little to comfort the woman as he made a desperate endeavour to make light of the situation; in fact, his tactless attempt to do so only seemed to increase her anger.

Drawing a steadying breath, Cordelia stepped forward in a vain attempt to retrieve the situation.

'I must apologise for my friend's over-exuberance,' she said.

Alex's grey eyes were impervious when they looked at her. 'I should think so. Of all the most stupid, irresponsible things to do. One would only expect such immature behaviour from children in a playground.'

Cordelia met his gaze, hot colour of indignation washing over her, finding it difficult to believe this was the same man who had engaged her in polite conversation earlier. 'Kindly have the courtesy to hear me out,' she said coldly. 'As you can see, my friends are celebrating. The unfortunate incident happened in just a harmless moment of fun.'

'Then let us be thankful not everyone here at Ascot today was as fortunate as your friend—otherwise we would all be awash with champagne,' Alex replied gratingly.

'Then it is a pity you did not partake of some yourself, sir, for I am certain it would have put you in better humour,' said Cordelia caustically.

'It seems to me there has been enough wine drunk in this vicinity to compensate for the rest of us.'

Cordelia lost her carefully controlled temper at his refusal to accept their apology. Her eyes sparkled with outrage. 'You really are quite insufferable and I am very sorry I ever tried to apologise to you.' She looked at the woman beside him who was visibly shaking with anger. 'I do hope your journey back to London won't be too uncomfortable,' she said stonily. 'And my friend was right. The day is unusually warm so I'm sure the heat will soon dry your dress.'

When Alex and his lady friend had passed on their way, high spirits were restored, the incident forgotten—by all but Cordelia, that is. The journey back to London passed on wings of laughter but Cordelia existed in a black void of anger mingled with humiliation over her third encounter with the man whose identity she still did not know.

Had she but known the unfortunate truth—that initially Alex had seen the funny side of the incident—her anger might not have been so acute.

On seeing the high and mighty self-assurance which Diana was in possession of at all times stripped away in such a comical fashion, Alex had had to restrain an impulse not to laugh. He had not felt like laughing in days and now, unfortunately, was not the time. To have done so would have provoked Diana to further anger at the humiliation heaped on her by the young revellers.

That had been Alex's first reaction to the incident, but it had changed quite dramatically, for the rush of resentment he had experienced when Miss King had quickly sprung to the defence of the fair-haired young man was quite ridiculous. But ridiculous or not, the admiration which had shone in the young man's eyes when he had looked at her told Alex that their relationship must be more than friendship.

Contrary to what Miss King thought, he did

understand the reasons for the young man's exuberance, who was still of an age when he had not learned the kind of control which comes with time and experience. Alex had suffered a feeling that was quite unfamiliar to him—jealousy—which was why a light-hearted situation had turned into an unpleasant incident, and his attitude had been derisive and cruel, which he now deeply regretted.

On the day of her interview Cordelia travelled by train to Norfolk, where she was met at the station by Lady McBride, who was to take her to Stanfield Hall, a large country house which had been used as a convalescent home for soldiers injured in the War.

The owner, Lord Frankland, a military gentleman—although his military rank of Captain had stuck with him, for almost everyone addressed him as Captain Frankland—now wanted it restoring to normal. Cordelia was to be interviewed for the position of secretary by Lady McBride herself, his aunt, who also lived at Stanfield Hall.

Having imagined someone who would resemble her mother, Cordelia was pleasantly surprised and relieved to discover Lady McBride was quite different. She thought she must be approaching sixty years of age, though still slender with a finely constructed bone structure. It was evident that she had once been a great beauty. She had the kind of natural elegance that most women strived for but could never achieve.

Her hair, which once must have been quite dark, was now streaked with silver. A long diaphanous scarf was wrapped around her head and drifted down her back, fluttering out like a pennant when she walked. Like her clothes, which were quite garish and unconventional, there was nothing subtle about Lady McBride as she chatted away nonstop all the way to Stanfield Hall, driving the car at such a madcap speed along the narrow lanes that Cordelia feared for her life.

Stanfield Hall was a welcoming, redbrick mansion at the end of a tree-enclosed approach, the handmade bricks having mellowed over the two centuries to a silvery pink.

Built in pleasing symmetry, it stood in perfect harmony against a backdrop of the heaths and pinewoods of Norfolk, with well-cultivated farmland and sea marshes to the east. Beyond the lawns around the house were gardens heavily planted with laurels and rhododendrons, and tall dark firs overshadowing ponds where water lilies strove to bloom in the gentle shade.

'Come inside, Miss King,' Lady McBride said, leading the way up the steps to the huge double doors. 'We can talk while we eat. I'm sure you must be ready for something after your journey.'

Cordelia followed her, a mixture of paint and carbolic assailing her nose when she entered the hallway, and had just enough time to admire its wealth of elaborate wood and plasterwork before being ushered into a small room leading off it, which was clearly used as an office. The surfaces of desks and chairs were cluttered with piles of papers and ledgers.

'As you can see,' said Lady McBride with a huge apologetic sigh, 'everything is in such a mess. Paperwork is not my strong point, which is why Stanfield is in dire need of a secretary.' She removed a pile of papers from one of the chairs. 'Come and sit down. I'll just go to the kitchen and see about some refreshment.'

Over a collation of cold meats and salad, Lady McBride quickly scanned Cordelia's qualifications, nodding in approval.

'Everything seems to be in order, Miss King,' she smiled. 'I congratulate you. Your qualifications from the secretarial college are excellent. You live in London, I understand?'

'Yes. I share a flat with a friend.'

'I see. And your family?'

'My family live in Yorkshire—near Leeds.'

'And your father? What is his occupation?'

'He is a businessman,' explained Cordelia, hoping Lady McBride would be satisfied with that and not ask any more questions concerning her family. She did not wish to reveal who her father was in case it jeopardised her chances of obtaining the position. It was so important to her self-esteem that she acquired it on merit. Thankfully Lady McBride stood up, seemingly satisfied with what Cordelia had told her.

'Well, Miss King, I am offering you the position as secretary here at Stanfield in the hope that you will accept. But, after you have seen the house and the enormity of the task involved, you may decide not to take it. Let me show you what it entails. We can talk as we go along.'

Restraining the glorious surge of euphoria which engulfed her at being offered the position so soon, Cordelia followed Lady McBride out into the hall.

'Stanfield Hall has sixty rooms, Miss King, and, like so many country houses during the war, was turned into a convalescent hospital, which it continued to be until just a few months ago. Some of the servants employed here before the war stayed on as nurses and porters. The patients who were able had free run of the house and gardens.

'Most of them loved it here,' she said, a softness filling her eyes and a warmth entering her voice as she remembered, 'and even now I get letters from some of the soldiers, telling me of their progress and how their lives have turned out now the War is over. Some of those men had been to hell and back, Miss King, and I am happy to say that Stanfield Hall played a very large part in the healing not only of their broken bodies but also of their minds and souls.'

'It's a lovely house,' said Cordelia. Familiar as she was with such large country houses, having been raised in one herself, this was the first she had seen that had been used as a hospital. 'I can see how they must have loved it here.'

'As you can see,' Lady McBride said, indicating the decorators' ladders and dust sheets thrown over huge pieces of furniture, 'there is much to be done in restoring it to what it once was. The attics and cellars—even the stables, which used to house some of the finest bloodstock in Norfolk—are piled high with stored furniture. The decorators have already begun their work and some of the estate workers are to assist in shifting the furniture.

'An inventory was done before everything was stored away. I do have the lists somewhere. The more valuable things, such as the silver and paintings and family heirlooms, were sent to London for safekeeping. No doubt my nephew will be arranging to have them returned whilst he is in London.'

'What will my work entail, Lady McBride, should I accept your offer?'

'Well,' she replied, looking at her directly in a forthright manner, 'for a start you will stop calling me Lady McBride. It's such a mouthful, I always think. You may call me Maxine. Everyone else does—even my nephew. Why should you be any different? And I will call you Delia—if that is acceptable to you?'

'Of course,' smiled Cordelia.

'Now—where to begin, that's the problem. Ah—the library, I think,' she said, entering a very large, high-ceilinged room with empty shelves lining the walls. 'Stanfield has a superb library. The books are all stored in the attics at present. You will be responsible for cataloguing, et cetera, after they have been oiled and aired by the servants.

'That is another thing,' she sighed, 'we'll have to get more staff—although domestics are difficult to get since the War. Most of the estate workers and the footmen who went to the War don't want to come back. I suppose they find life in the big wide world more amusing than being in service.'

What Lady McBride said was true in the case of most large country houses. Cordelia remembered her mother say how difficult it was to get staff at Edenthorpe since the War.

'Also,' Lady McBride continued, 'in the absence of a housekeeper, all the linen will have to be checked and listed—but don't worry,' she laughed, on seeing Cordelia's bemused look, 'that is a task I shall undertake myself—when I get around to it—like a thousand and one other tasks waiting to be done.

'Of course, Captain Frankland—whose mother was my sister, and died just before the War, which was when I came to live at Stanfield, having already lost my own husband—wants changes made. Modernised was the word he used, which is perfectly natural, I suppose, when younger people take over. He wants the dark paint and lavish clutter that his parents and grandparents so delighted in replaced by lighter colours and less crowded rooms.

'Because the house has been used as a hospital, you will soon discover there are several bathrooms. Also, while the house is in such an upheaval, my nephew thought it a good idea to have the new electric lights installed. It's rather extravagant—especially because of the high taxes imposed on us since the War, but there it is. Although Alex will have little time to supervise what is happening in the house when he returns, I'm afraid—he will have his work cut out running the estate.'

'Is there no agent at Stanfield Hall to handle the management of the estate?' asked Cordelia, thinking of her father's agent at Edenthorpe who managed all estate affairs, leaving her father free to involve himself in other matters.

'No. There was before the War but, like a lot more people, he left to join up. No doubt my nephew will appoint one eventually, but until he does then we have to manage as best we can.'

'Who would be my employer?'

'Why, my nephew, of course.'

'And is Captain Frankland a married gentleman?'

A veil seemed to descend over Lady McBride's features. 'He was. His wife, Pamela, was killed in the War during an air raid on London.'

'Oh—I'm so sorry. I—I did not mean to pry.'

'No—of course you didn't,' she smiled. 'But, anyhow, it's as well you know. After all, in addition to helping me put the house to rights, you will also be my nephew's personal secretary. Do you know anything about art, by the way?'

'I do have some knowledge,' Cordelia replied truthfully, for her governess had educated her, as she had her sisters before her, to be reasonably well versed in the arts, English and mathematics.

'Good. My nephew is extremely interested in the subject—although horses are his first love. He is a typical sportsman in the hunting field and racing circles. And that is another thing. No doubt he will want to begin filling the stables the minute he returns.'

'Captain Frankland will be expecting to find me here when he arrives, won't he?'

'Why—yes.'

'And he will have no aversion to my being a woman?' she asked carefully.

'Gracious me—I haven't thought about that. Does it matter?'

'Well—yes. You see, there are still a great many people who are against women working.'

'That may be—but women should not be denied skills because of their gender. I'm all for it, I can tell you. I nursed the wounded during the War—drove an ambulance, even. Some women joined the WACs and went to France to work in the hospitals. They saw the worst that could happen. Women are no longer innocents so why should they withdraw their services and retreat into the old restrictive practices of before the War? Have you heard of women's suffrage, Delia?'

'Of course.'

'Well, now we have the vote at long last—thanks to women like Mrs Pankhurst—there will be no going back. Although we will not be entirely satisfied until we have it on equal terms with men and the age is brought down from thirty to twenty-one.'

'And Captain Frankland? Is he of the same opinion?'

Maxine smiled, a glint of mischief in her eyes. 'Dear me, no. Quite the opposite, in fact.'

Cordelia's heart plummeted when she began to realise what she would be up against. 'Then, when he returns to Stanfield Hall, might he not wish to dismiss me?'

'He might—but you leave that for me to worry about. My nephew might know what he's about when he's with the army and he thinks he's dealing with subordinates, but when dealing with me he knows I can be as formidable as any commanding officer.'

Cordelia did not doubt that for one moment. 'And when will Captain Frankland be returning to Stanfield Hall?'

'In two weeks' time, I believe. He's recently been on holiday in France, but at the moment he's in London where he has rather a lot of business to attend to before returning to Stanfield.' She looked at Cordelia directly. Capable of summing people up at a glance, Maxine had already developed a liking for Delia King. 'So tell me, does the position as secretary to my nephew appeal to you?'

Cordelia smiled. 'Yes—thank you. I would like it very much.'

Maxine sighed with relief. At last she had someone to help shoulder some of the workload. 'Good. Then that is settled. I will take you upstairs and show you the room you will occupy for the time beings. If it isn't to your liking, it can always be changed when others have been decorated. Now—how soon can you start?'

'When would you like me to start?'

'Monday?'

Cordelia nodded. 'Yes.'

'The sooner the better. You should have time to settle in before my nephew arrives. When he sees you are already established it will be harder for him to kick up a fuss. With two women at the helm to contend with,' she chuckled, 'instead of just the one, he may consider hotfooting it back to the army. Poor Alex. He doesn't know what he's in for.'

Neither did Cordelia. If she had, she might never have returned to Stanfield Hall.

Cordelia began work at Stanfield Hall on the following Monday as arranged and, in no time at all, made herself indispensable to Maxine, with a competence that amazed the older woman. She set about helping to restore the house with an alarming capability, possessing a flair for arranging things with an eye for colour which led Maxine to suspect she must have been born to life within an establishment such as Stanfield.

With the inventory in her hand she began by systematically making a tour of the house, starting with the attics, which were piled high with furniture, chests of outmoded clothes, books, and pictures that had to be cleaned and rehung in the places they had occupied before the house had been turned into a convalescent hospital.

The work was hardly what she had been trained for or expected, but that would come later when Captain Frankland returned. Nevertheless, she was enjoying it and liked working alongside Maxine. At the end of the first week, when she returned to London for the weekend, she was shattered, but by Sunday evening she was ready to return, driving back to Norfolk in her car.

The sun was just beginning to set in a line of crimson on the horizon when she was close to Stanfield Hall, the trees and hedgerows on either side of the narrow road passing by in a haze, the wheels of her car whipping up dust and leaves in its wake.

The road turned suddenly, causing her to corner hard, when suddenly she found herself confronted by a horse, standing immobile in the middle of the road. She hit the brakes hard, which caused her to skid to one side; on trying to correct it, she slipped almost gracefully into a ditch at the side of the road.

Unhurt, still holding the steering wheel, she sat for a moment to recover from the shock before reaching out and switching off the ignition. She looked about her. The inquisitive horse came to put its head over the door of the car, blinking its big dark eyes and nuzzling Cordelia's shoulder with its velvety nostrils, its rich dark coat rippling in the shadows.

She knew she should be angry with the horse, a beautiful black stallion with a white blaze, but she couldn't. It had no saddle or bridle, so she thought it must have got out of a field somewhere. Reaching out, she ran her hands over his sleek coat.

'You are so beautiful,' she said, 'but we'll have to find out where you've come from.'

Cordelia climbed out of the car, wondering how on earth she was going to get the car, which she hoped would be undamaged, out of the ditch. The side she could see looked all right but she could not be sure about the other until it had been pulled out.

Beginning to lead the horse up the road, suddenly she stopped; she could hear a car approaching from the direction in which she had just come. Standing to one side to let it pass, it was not until it came round the corner that she saw it was a familiar yellow and black Daimler.

Cordelia's eyes opened wide in amazement. She watched as the car pulled off the road onto the grass verge where it came to a halt, the driver silencing the engine and climbing out. At that moment Cordelia wished the ground would open and swallow her up, but there was no escape.

Also returning from London, Alex paused to look at her car teetering in the ditch before walking boldly up to her, his limp barely noticeable. His eyes were drawn by the pale, graceful figure on the side of the road.

He wore a white shirt, casually open at the throat, and dark trousers. A last lingering ray of sunlight filtered through the branches of one of the trees at the side of the road, shining on his sleek black hair drawn back from his smooth forehead, serving to set off his incredibly handsome good looks.

Cordelia gazed at him, so surprised at seeing him that she was unable to get a word out. What she was not expecting was the sudden quickening of her heart when he stopped in front of her with that look of recognition and cynical amusement in his eyes. She met his gaze unwillingly, with growing annoyance that he should be here to witness her calamity.

'I thought I recognised your car. You have a peculiar habit of turning up in the most surprising places, Miss King.'

Cordelia stiffened her spine when she remembered the unpleasantness of their last meeting at Ascot and her eyes clouded suddenly, her mouth becoming set in a hard line.

'And, of all people, *you* have to turn up.'

'And, it would seem, right on cue,' he said glancing back at her car. 'You seem to be having a spot of trouble.'

'Nothing I can't deal with,' she said ungraciously.

'I'm sure you're more than capable of dealing with most things, but I doubt even you could pull your car out of that ditch unaided. Are you all right? You are not hurt?'

'No,' she replied, touched by his note of concern. 'Perhaps a little shaken at first, but that's all.'

Alex observed the horse nibbling unconcernedly at the grass. 'Did he cause you to swerve off the road?'

'Yes. I didn't see him until it was too late. He must have got out of a field somewhere. I was just about to walk along the road to see if a gate had been left open.'

'That's more than likely. There's a pasture further along where a neighbour of mine often grazes his horses. You stay here and I'll take him. Come along, old boy,' he said, grasping a handful of mane and beginning to lead the horse along the road.

Cordelia watched him go, wondering what to make of the situation. He had said the horse probably belonged to a neighbour of his; if this was the case, then it was highly likely he lived nearby and she would see him again. When he returned, she was standing beside her car, trying to work out how she was going to retrieve it from the ditch.

'You were right—a gate had been left open. I've secured it so he won't get out so easily a second time. I think you'd better come with me,' he said. 'When we get to the house I'll send someone with the proper equipment to pull it out.'

'No—I couldn't possibly,' she said tersely, the thought of being alone with him for any length of time strangely disconcerting.

'I insist,' he said in a tone which told her he would brook no nonsense. 'Being a gentleman—

which you are at liberty to dispute if you wish—I cannot leave you here alone. Shall we call a truce until your car has been retrieved and you have continued on your way? Come now—you cannot deny me my act of chivalry.'

In spite of her annoyance over his behaviour on their previous encounters, Cordelia found herself smiling.

'Ah—you see—you can smile. You should do it more often. Anger does not become you.'

'Far be it from me to object to any chivalrous inclinations you may have—so—it seems I will have to accept.'

'Thank goodness. Now come along. If we're to have your car back on the road before dark, then we'll have to get a move on.'

Forced to admit defeat, not relishing the long walk to Stanfield alone to get help, Cordelia did as she was told and climbed into his car. For a moment there was silence between them as they sped along the road, which Cordelia was the first to break. Meeting his gaze squarely as he cast her a sidelong glance, she took a deep breath.

'Thank you for not making some flippant comment about finding my car in the ditch.'

The merest ghost of a smile touched his mouth. 'Had I not seen the horse and drawn my own conclusion as to what had happened, I might have been tempted,' he admitted, 'but I am not so insensitive. It would seem that apologies are the order of the day,' he said softly, fixing his eyes on the road ahead.

Cordelia looked across at him in some surprise. 'Why? What are you saying?'

'My lack of self-control at Ascot. It was inexcusable,' he said, making a gesture of self-reproach. 'I was not at my best that day.'

'Evidently.'

'I do improve on acquaintance,' he murmured, his eyes twinkling across at her.

'Probably—and I suppose the same could be said of rattlesnakes and such like—but that does not mean one has to like them. However,' she smiled, 'your lack of self-control was not unreasonable. Had someone soaked me with champagne I would have behaved exactly the same as—' She glanced at him enquiringly. 'What was the lady's name?'

'Miss Hibbert.'

'Miss Hibbert. She had cause to be angry.'

Alex smiled across at her, a singularly attractive smile, that took Cordelia unawares and had an unsettling effect on her.

'It is good of you to say so. Tell me, Miss King, what are you doing in Norfolk? Are you visiting someone?'

'No. I work here.'

'Work?'

'Yes. Work.' She looked at him sideways. 'Is there something wrong with that?'

'No, of course not. It's just that you do not seem to be the type.'

'Oh—and what type do you think I am?'

'Certainly not the type who has to earn a living. You drive a car for one thing, and my experienced eye observes you wear expensive clothes. You must hold a responsible position to be able to afford it.'

'Not that it is any of your concern,' she said, 'but my car I bought out of a legacy left to me by my grandmother.'

Alex nodded. 'I see—then that explains it. Is your home in London?'

'No. In the north. I share a flat in Bloomsbury with a friend of mine.'

'Don't tell me,' he grinned, turning his head and looking at her, 'but you pay for it out of your grandmother's legacy.'

'Yes. Something like that.'

'Your grandmother must have been extremely wealthy.'

'Yes—she was—quite rich.'

'What was she like—your grandmother?'

'Oh—small and wrinkled—with white hair. Isn't everyone's grandmother?'

'No. Mine was quite different,' he smiled.

'You must live close to here,' said Cordelia, curious to know more about him.

'Yes—not far.'

At that moment Cordelia saw they were

approaching Stanfield Hall and was just about to ask him to slow down, that it would be just as easy for her to send someone out from Stanfield Hall to retrieve her car, when he swung in through the wrought-iron gates and proceeded on up the drive.

'As soon as we get to Stanfield—that's my home,' he explained, totally unaware of the shock waves shooting through her as terrible, unthinkable suspicions began forming in her mind, 'I'll send someone to pull your car out.'

Cordelia stared at him in horror. No, it couldn't be who she thought it was. That was absurd. Her mouth had gone suddenly dry. 'Stanfield! Then—then you are—'

'Alex Frankland. I own Stanfield Hall.'

Chapter Four

As the car slithered to a halt at the bottom of the steps leading up to the house, a numbness rendered Cordelia motionless. For a moment she simply stared at Alex Frankland, and then, because Maxine chose that moment to come out of the house to welcome her nephew home, she was prevented from having any further conversation. Alex climbed out to embrace the woman on the steps while Cordelia remained where she was inside the car, all the doors to understanding finally becoming wide open.

She closed her eyes. She knew that once Captain Frankland found out she was working for him it would be the signing of her death warrant. She knew as she hesitated before getting out of the car that she was hoping for some last-minute rescue from her dilemma—but she was hoping in vain.

Slowly she climbed out of the car. When she saw his handsome smile—and, as always when he looked at her, that glimmer of amusement in his eyes—she asked herself how long it would last when he knew who she was. At that moment she had a natural reluctance for him to know what she was doing at Stanfield Hall.

'Why—Delia,' said Maxine in surprise on seeing her coming towards them. 'Oh—so you two have met. I'm so glad.'

'Yes,' Cordelia replied with tension in her voice when she looked at her employer, 'but we have not been formally introduced.'

Alex's face had taken on a bemused look.

'Alex—this is Miss Delia King,' explained Maxine. 'She is your new secretary.'

Cordelia watched his expression as if to assess the effect of this bombshell. He became quite, quite still and his face settled into harsh lines as his eyes impaled her like sharp flints.

'Well, well,' he said icily. 'And I am expected to comply with this?'

'Yes, you are,' retorted Maxine in a tone which told him she would tolerate no argument. 'Miss King has been at Stanfield for a week now and has proved to be quite indispensable. I could not possibly manage without her.'

Beginning to see everything she had worked for about to shatter into smithereens, anger stirred inside Cordelia.

'Please—excuse me,' she said in a voice shaking with temper, which neither of them could fail to be aware of. 'I'll leave you to explain, Maxine. I'll go and find Thomas to see what can be done about getting my car out of the ditch. I'm going to need it if I'm to return to London.'

'Ditch? What ditch? What is all this?' asked Maxine, looking from one to the other.

'I encountered Miss King further down the road,' explained Alex. 'Her car had run into a ditch.'

Maxine was suddenly filled with concern. 'Are you all right, Delia? You're not hurt?'

'No, I'm fine,' Cordelia reassured her. 'I had to swerve to avoid a horse standing in the middle of the road.'

'I see. Thank goodness you were not hurt. So—you have only just met—and here I was thinking you had travelled from London together.'

'As a matter of fact, our paths have crossed before,' drawled Alex. 'Twice, in fact, although we were unaware of each other's identity at that time. I have to say that neither meeting was fortuitous.' His eyes fastened on Cordelia. 'Please excuse me if I do not seem overjoyed with the situation imposed on me by my dear aunt, but this is all a surprise to me.'

'And clearly a disagreeable one,' said Cordelia tersely. 'I'll go and find Thomas. Excuse me.' She turned abruptly and walked away in the direction of the stables where she knew Thomas, the general handyman at Stanfield, could be found, leaving them staring at her retreating back.

Maxine began walking back into the house followed by her irate nephew.

'Maxine?'

'What is it?' she replied, walking towards the office.

'Miss King.'

'What about Miss King?'

'When I asked you to employ someone I did not expect—'

'What?' asked Maxine, turning to face him, completely unfazed by his anger. 'I don't remember you saying anything about employing someone of the male sex, Alex, and for the life of me I cannot see why you think it necessary to make all this fuss. Miss King is more than qualified for the job in hand. We are extremely lucky to have her. Besides, she was the only one who applied for the position who was interested in taking on such a mammoth task.'

'Nevertheless, I did not expect you to employ a woman.'

'And what is wrong with a woman wanting to work, might I ask? Women worked during the War and were extremely good at it, too.'

'That was different,' he argued stubbornly, having been caught in a situation he did not know how to deal with.

'Why is it, for heaven's sake? Miss King may have been born in a male-dominated age, when women were kept at home imprisoned by their menfolk to do mundane tasks such as cleaning, cooking and rearing a child year in and year out—but clearly that was not what she wanted and did something about it. I admire her for that, Alex. It cannot have been easy for her.

'Her skills as a secretary are excellent and—why, she can read a balance sheet better than any man I know. Give her a chance. After the sterling work women like her did during the War, you and men like you, with the power to improve their lot in life, owe them that.'

Sighing, Alex looked into his aunt's eyes and he was lost. She always knew how to defeat him. Initially he had been resolutely against allowing Miss King to remain at Stanfield in the capacity of his secretary. Yet, at the back of his mind, he did not want to see her go—she had already begun to twine her fine, delicate fingers around his heart.

Besides, what logical reason did he have to ask her to leave? He could not hold the fact that she was a woman against her—not that he had anything in general against women, it was just that he never thought he would have to work in such close proximity with one—and Maxine had said what a fine secretary she was.

'Besides,' smiled Maxine, her eyes twinkling with mischief, 'you must have noticed that she's prettier than I am. Won't it be much nicer looking across a desk at her in the mornings instead of an old woman like me?'

Alex's gaze swept fondly over her face. 'You'll never be old, Maxine, and you know it. All right—you win. Send Miss King in to see me before she packs her bags and returns to London. But, whatever you say, I believe her to be one of the new liberated women taking a job of work for the fun of it—and I am fully convinced she won't last longer than a fortnight.'

Maxine smiled tolerantly. 'Then for once, Alex, I believe you are about to be proved wrong—and I shall enjoy watching Delia prove you wrong.'

Cordelia and Alex were in the office alone. In a state of cold apprehension she waited for him to speak; he punished her with a long silence. What she expected to hear was that she was to be dismissed before she had even started her work properly. Although she knew she should feel relieved that she might have to leave Stanfield and would not have to work for him, something she could not identify shifted behind her ribs. Unable to stand the silence a moment longer, she took the initiative.

'It is clear to me that you do not like the situation any more than I do,' she said quietly. 'If I'd had any idea who you were, I would never have applied for the position. But the fact is that I did—and I am sorry if my being here has caused you any embarrassment—so I think it is best that I leave.'

'That is defeatist talk, Miss King. At first, when I realised what Maxine had done, I may have been a bit hasty. I apologise.'

Cordelia stared at him with some surprise. 'Are you saying that I can stay?'

'Yes, that is what I am saying.'

She sighed with genuine relief. 'Thank you. That is extremely generous of you.'

'Generosity has nothing to do with it. I need a secretary and someone to help Maxine put the house to rights. You applied for the position and were successful in obtaining it. So—welcome to Stanfield Hall, Miss King. I shall look forward to working with you.'

His expression was so bland that Cordelia had no way of knowing whether he meant what he said or not—but she was relieved to know she didn't have to return to London to begin looking for another position. 'Thank you. I would be sorry to have to leave. You won't regret it—I promise you.'

'No. I don't believe I will,' he said softly.

Cordelia hadn't expected him to trust her with the colossal task of helping to put Stanfield to rights, but she would show him. She would work night and day if need be to prove her worth.

'By the way,' he said as she was about to leave,

'my name is Alex. If we are to work together it might be better if we dropped formalities between us.'

'I disagree. If you don't mind, I would prefer to address you as Captain Frankland. If we are to work so closely together, then it is always as well that some kind of barrier remains between employer and employee. Goodnight, Captain Frankland.'

'As you wish. Goodnight, Miss King.'

Although Alex would never confess as much to Maxine, over the following weeks he was pleasantly surprised and extremely impressed by Cordelia's work, which could not be faulted, but he was finding it increasingly difficult to ignore the fact that she was a very desirable woman.

When she sat at her desk, so prim, with a look of absorbed concentration on her face and her head bent over the ledgers, he noticed the soft curve of her cheek and the long silky sweep of her eyelashes. Often he would find himself dwelling on her shining cap of golden hair and hazel eyes, bright and alert as she went about her work.

Without doubt she was one of the most beautiful women he had ever seen. She was also capable and intelligent and extremely efficient at her work, treating him with a cool, businesslike formality, her face always set in a mould of politeness. In fact, she was the perfect secretary.

It was good to see Maxine not having to work so hard. He always tried to keep the conversation neutral and was forever cautious not to overstep the line that separated employer from employee. But this was becoming increasingly more difficult.

Cordelia enjoyed her work and Maxine's companionship, although since Alex's return to Stanfield her workload had increased considerably, which she took in her stride. She knew he was driving her hard to see how far he could push her before she was forced to admit defeat, but she did not show it and was somewhat amused by it.

In between Alex visiting horse sales up and down the country in his desire to fill Stanfield's stables with fine horses, and spending time in London, there were days when Cordelia rarely saw him at all, and it was during these times that, despite all the work that needed to be done, she became acutely conscious of how much she missed him when he was away.

She often found her thoughts dwelling on his dead wife, Pamela—wondering what she had been like. She found it strange that no one ever mentioned her. There were no photographs, nothing to suggest he'd ever had a wife—perhaps the reason being that it was too painful for him to be reminded of her.

However, whatever the reason for the mystery surrounding her, she could not help being curious about her, but kept her thoughts to herself. It was, after all, nothing to do with her.

She also found her thoughts turning to the beautiful Diana Hibbert whom she had seen Alex with at Ascot, who had clung to his side with a possessiveness accorded to a fiancée or a wife. Was their relationship a close one? she asked herself. Did he spend most of his time with her when he went to London?

She rebuked herself angrily for thinking thoughts like these. Captain Frankland might be a very attractive man but she was not going to allow herself to fall into any kind of emotional trap over him. Their relationship was a strictly working one and that was how it would remain.

It was on her arrival back at Stanfield Hall one Sunday evening, after spending her weekend in London with Kitty, that Cordelia saw a shiny black Bentley parked in the drive. Suspecting that Alex must have visitors and not wishing to intrude, she picked up her travelling bag, intending to go straight to her room unobserved.

Alex had been entertaining James Hibbert and his sister Diana for the day at Stanfield Hall. Originally he had invited James up from London to see two horses he'd bought at the Doncaster horse sales the previous week but, to his irritation, Diana had arrived with him. She was seated on the large sofa in the centre of the room, sipping a cocktail, her long legs elegantly crossed in front of her and smoking a cigarette through a long cigarette holder.

Alex was standing by the window looking out when Cordelia pulled up in her little white car in front of the house, looking delectable in a short, straight pink dress.

'I think we had better be getting back to London, Alex,' said James. 'It will soon be dark and it's a long drive.'

He joined Alex at the window, and whistled softly in appreciation when he saw Cordelia climbing out of her car.

'I say, who is that gorgeous creature getting out of that car?'

'Miss King—my secretary.'

Diana's attention was caught and she looked across at them sharply. James stared at him in amazement.

'Secretary? You've been keeping her under wraps, haven't you, Alex?'

They watched as Cordelia climbed out of her car, coming round to the passenger door and reaching inside for her bag, unknowingly giving both James and Alex a glimpse of her long, slender legs.

'Good Lord, Alex—she's stunning—although,' he said, frowning slightly, 'she does look vaguely familiar. Still—I must be mistaken. I can't have seen her before because I'd never forget a face as lovely as that.' James couldn't take his eyes off her. 'How can you possibly concentrate on work with someone like that around?'

'It's quite simple, James,' laughed Alex. 'We're not all lecherous reprobates like you.'

'How the hell did you get hold of a girl like that?'

'I didn't. Maxine did. I had no say on the matter. When I returned from London, Miss King was well established at Stanfield and already indispensable. Since then I have to admit that she is proving to be an extremely capable and intelligent young woman. I could hardly ask her to leave.'

'And who in their right mind would want her to? I say—ask her in for a drink, Alex, there's a good chap. Be nice to be introduced before we have to leave.'

'Whenever Miss King returns to Stanfield after her weekend off she always goes straight to her room. She will not be seen until morning. She makes her own rules and adheres to them rigidly.'

'Rules are made to be broken.' James winked and smiled wickedly. 'Perhaps tonight she'll make an exception—if you were to ask her nicely, that is. If you won't, I will.'

Persuaded, Alex sighed. 'All right—I'll go and ask her. But don't say I didn't warn you if she refuses.'

He went out into the hall and met Cordelia as she was about to climb the stairs.

'Miss King?'

Cordelia turned and looked at him, her heart giving a little flutter of elation on seeing him. She waited for him to speak.

'I have friends in the drawing-room who are shortly to leave for London.'

'I thought you must have. I saw their car in the drive.'

'James insisted I invite you in for a drink. Would you care to join us?'

'That's extremely kind of you, but I would not wish to intrude.'

'You wouldn't be intruding. Come along. I'll introduce you—although I think I should warn you that Diana you've already met,' he said, catching her eye with a meaningful smile. 'At Ascot. I believe your friend thought she was rather partial to champagne.'

Cordelia met his gaze with cynical amusement. 'Oh—yes. I remember her—and that unfortunate incident well.' She smiled. 'Oh, dear. I feel a bit like Daniel must have felt upon entering the lion's den.'

'And it wasn't anything like he'd imagined it to be.'

'Yes—God saved him, as I remember it. Who's going to save me?'

Alex chuckled softly. 'I'll do my best. Come along,' he said, taking her elbow. 'James saw you arrive and won't be satisfied until he knows everything about you.'

'Everything?' murmured Cordelia, looking up at him sideways with a little quirk to her lips.

He grinned. 'Well—almost everything.'

The minute Cordelia stepped inside the room James was smitten. Her soft femininity and boyish looks captivated his attention immediately. Beaming broadly, he moved towards her.

'James—may I introduce my secretary, Miss King.'

James scowled at Alex. 'I say—Miss King! That's a bit formal, isn't it?'

Alex's lips curled in a smile when he caught Cordelia's amused eye. 'She will not have it any other way, will you, Miss King?'

'Ah—but I'm not her employer—so maybe she'll allow me to be less formal and have a drink with me before I have to fly off to London. So—what do I call you?' he asked.

With his fair hair and winning smile, Cordelia warmed to the admiration in James's blue eyes and laughed lightly. 'Delia—and yes, please—I'd love a drink.'

'Have we met somewhere before, Delia? I was telling Alex when we saw you getting out of your car that your face seems vaguely familiar.'

Sudden panic caused Cordelia's heart to skip a beat but somehow she managed to remain calm and keep smiling. She certainly couldn't remember seeing him before, but if he had chanced to see her at a party somewhere then it would have been before she'd had her long hair cut short, which had changed her appearance somewhat.

'I very much doubt it. Before coming to work at Stanfield Hall, my social life had been at a stand-still for quite some time. All my efforts were concentrated on qualifying to become a secretary. Unless, of course, you happened to see me at Ascot on Ladies Day—the day I bumped into Captain Frankland.'

James nodded. It was possible that this could be the explanation as to why she looked familiar. 'Yes—that must be it.' He looked at his sister as she stepped forward. 'This is Diana—my sister, by the way.'

Relieved that James had accepted her explanation as to where he might have seen her before, Cordelia faced Diana, remembering all too vividly their last meeting and the anger and humiliation she had suffered when Jeremy had soaked her in champagne. She noticed her finely moulded features and her eyes, narrow and dark, beneath thin, pencilled, arched brows. There was a bitter twist to her lips and she looked at Cordelia slightly contemptuously.

'Yes, we have met before,' said Diana, her voice low and as smooth as silk. 'At Ascot. It is an occasion I do not care to be reminded of.'

'Then we will not mention it,' said Cordelia politely.

As before, when they had met at Ascot, she sensed instant antagonism when she looked into Diana's dark eyes—and when she saw the covetous way she clung to Alex's side she knew why. It was perfectly natural she would resent Cordelia's own relationship with him—even if it was a working one—for she would feel her own relationship under threat.

Cordelia took a glass of wine from Alex and sipped it gratefully, meeting his eyes over the rim of the glass.

'Alex has just been telling us of your capabilities, Delia,' said James, 'that you have become quite indispensable at Stanfield. High praise, I assure you, from a man who does not sing one's praises lightly. So you see, there is little wonder I wanted to make your acquaintance.'

Cordelia turned her head and surveyed Alex thoughtfully. 'It is always nice to know one is appreciated.'

'Of course you are, Miss King. Maxine would be at a loss to know what to do without you.'

There was dancing mockery in his eyes and a smile lurking in hers.

'She was managing quite well before I came. I'm sure she would do so again.'

'I can see I shall have to pay another visit to Stanfield quite soon, Alex,' James said, 'only the next time it will not be to look at horses—unless, of course—you ride, Delia?'

'Yes, I do ride.'

'Then that is settled. Is that all right with you, Alex?'

'Of course. Although Miss King does not need to ask my permission. What she does outside working hours is entirely her own affair.'

'Do you live in London?' James asked her.

'Yes. I share a flat with a friend of mine in Bloomsbury.'

'Then on one of your weekends off maybe you would care to dine with me?'

Cordelia did not look at Alex, but she was vividly conscious of him standing there. 'Yes—thank you. I'd like that,' she said, finding his vitality and easy charm quite infectious, although she suspected that with his immodest, natural, fun loving spirit, the minute he had left her company he would have forgotten his offer.

'I think we should be going, James,' said Diana, stony-faced. 'We don't want to arrive in London too late.'

'Yes—all right. Although I'm beginning to wish we didn't have to leave,' he said, looking at Cordelia with mock solemnity at having to leave such charming company.

After seeing his guests off, Alex returned to the drawing-room where Cordelia had just finished her drink and was about to go to her room.

'Please—stay and have another glass of wine

with me before you go rushing off to your room. I would like to talk to you,' he said, refilling her glass before she had time to object, for he was reluctant to let her go. He had never seen her sparkle as she had when in James's presence, which had made him feel uneasy. He had not been at all pleased at the effect she'd had on his friend.

'Thank you,' she replied, 'although I mustn't stay too long. I do have quite a lot to do before morning.'

'Yes—I'm sure you do.'

A faint smile touched Cordelia's lips when she looked to where he sat across from her, a scowl marring his handsome features. 'Do I detect a hint of sarcasm in that remark, Captain Frankland?' she asked softly.

'Not at all. It's just that whilst you've been at Stanfield I haven't seen you relax much. I hope we're not working you too hard?'

'No—but there is a lot to do.'

'Not so much that you can't take time off. Although I have to say you've worked wonders with the house. The work has progressed much faster than I envisaged. The decorators will soon have finished. I do believe I have you to thank for that. Also the office work has never been in such excellent order, although I'm aware what a difficult task this is. Unfortunately, because of high taxation, many landowners like myself are having to tighten their belts.'

Cordelia knew this to be true because her father was experiencing the same difficulties.

'I'm thinking of making changes on the estate—introducing new farming methods and perhaps some new breeds of cattle. Hopefully it might help to make the land more profitable. However, enough shop talk, Miss King. It has been rather remiss of me not to ask what you do for recreation.'

'Oh—I read quite a lot and listen to the wireless—go for walks with Maxine. And then there are my weekends in London with Kitty. I can honestly say I haven't the time to be bored.'

'And your family? Do you find time to visit them on your weekends away from Stanfield?'

'No—at least not recently,' she said, lowering her gaze, a slight tremor entering her voice. 'I—I shall have to take a few days off though, next month. My sister is getting married, you see.'

'That shouldn't be a problem,' said Alex, curious as to why she should look so ill at ease when he had mentioned her family. 'By the way—I meant what I said to James. You must feel free to ride any time you wish. Now I have started replenishing the stables with some decent mounts, I am sure you will find something suitable to ride. I'll sort something out for you first thing in the morning.'

'That's kind of you.'

'Not at all. You'll be doing me a favour. As you know, horses need plenty of exercise.'

'So,' she laughed jokingly, 'am I to add the position of groom to my other duties?'

'If you like. But I think you'll look on it as a pleasant one. As James is not here to accompany you, then I may do so myself on occasion. What did you think of James, by the way?'

'Is he always so exuberant and easy with his charms?'

'Always. Wherever he goes it's the same story. His popularity is quite sensational—which, unfortunately for his friends, has a stimulating effect on him. Fatigue is a word he is not familiar with. He is fabulously wealthy, his passion being for horses, and when he is not living at his home in Leicestershire or enjoying the high life in London, he goes to Rouen in France where he has a chateau. Whenever he is there, his neighbours spend days preparing elaborate and expensive parties in his honour.'

'And his sister Diana?' Cordelia asked tentatively, having noticed there had been nothing lover-like in Alex's behaviour towards Diana when she had observed him giving her just a platonic farewell peck on the cheek on her departure for London—although she suspected Diana would very much have preferred it to have been a kiss on her lips. 'Does she live with him?'

'Yes.' His eyes narrowed as he watched her

closely and she sensed a change in his mood. 'You made quite an impression on James, Miss King. I have a feeling he will be paying us a visit here at Stanfield quite soon.'

'I—I'm sure you're quite mistaken,' Cordelia said hesitantly, trying to make light of what he was implying. 'Why—the moment he gets to London and some other female catches his eye, he will have forgotten all about your ordinary, uninteresting secretary.'

Something flared in Alex's intense gaze and he managed a faintly crooked smile, his eyes lingering on the soft contours of her mouth. 'That is not how others see you. There is certainly nothing ordinary or uninteresting about you, Miss King. Take my word for it,' he said softly. 'You may always appear self-assured—but I suspect that beneath your cool façade hidden fires burn.'

Hot colour flooded Cordelia's face and suddenly she felt bemused. Alex was looking at her penetratingly, as though he were trying to discover what she was thinking. She stood up, placing her half-empty glass on the occasional table beside her, lowering her gaze as she tried to shake off the effect he was beginning to have on her.

'You—you shouldn't say such things. You seem to forget that you are my employer.'

Alex sighed, also rising. 'Forget? How can I forget when you remind me of it whenever we find ourselves together? Not by word, I admit, but by your manner.'

'I am sorry. I don't mean to. But it has to be this way. You do understand, don't you?'

'Do I have a choice? You are an extremely fascinating young woman. You intrigue me!'

'And you are a man of the world, Captain Frankland. I am your secretary and by speaking to me like this you must realise you are making it very difficult for me. Both you and your friend James Hibbert are wasting your time if you think I am an easy conquest. I am far from it, I can assure you. Now, I must go,' she said quickly. 'Thank you so much for the wine.'

'If you must,' he said, coming to stand beside her, then moving with her towards the door. Before she could disappear into the hall he lightly caught her arm and turned her to face him. Cordelia was not small, but he was taller by five or six inches and she had to look up at him. 'There is something I have to say to you before you go.'

Cordelia's eyes were held by his penetrating gaze and she felt a tightening in her throat. He was standing so close that she thought he was going to kiss her. She felt alarmed, more so when she realised that it was not of him she was afraid, but of herself. Why had she allowed herself to get into this situation? She should have declined his invitation to meet James Hibbert and his sister and gone straight to her room.

'What is it?' she asked, surprised at hearing her voice sound normal.

'Maxine has decided to visit friends in Eastbourne for a while. Has she mentioned this to you?'

'No. I knew she was considering taking a holiday, but I thought it would not be until later in the year. How long does she intend being away?'

'Two or three weeks, I believe. I know this is a pretty hectic time and that, because of her absence, more work will be thrust onto your shoulders, but with all the upheaval here at Stanfield in recent months she is beginning to look tired. I do believe some time spent away from here with her friends will be good for her. Of course, I shall be here to help—although during the time she will be away there are several horse sales I wish to visit, and I would like you to accompany me.'

Cordelia looked at him with some surprise; he had never suggested she accompany him before. 'Oh!' she exclaimed. 'Will that be necessary?'

'As you never cease to remind me, Miss King, I am your employer. This is not a suggestion or an invitation. It is all part of the work I wish you to do for me. There is nothing irregular in this; I have decided I need my secretary with me to take care of any paperwork, should I wish to purchase a horse.' He paused for a moment, looking into her troubled eyes, sensing that the reason for this was that they would be alone together.

'When Maxine has left for Eastbourne I do realise we will be alone at Stanfield—apart from the servants, of course. Clearly we will be thrown together a great deal—but let me put your mind at rest by saying that I promise to behave like a perfect gentleman at all times. Not once will I forget that you are my employee. So what do you say? Do you have any objections?'

Cordelia stared at him, taken completely by surprise. 'Why—no—of course I haven't—only I must be home for my sister's wedding.' If she wasn't, she thought, her mother would never forgive her. 'If Maxine isn't back before then—then I'm afraid I'll have to ask for a few days off.'

'When is the wedding?'

'A month from now.'

'Don't worry. Maxine will be back at Stanfield long before then.' His seriousness of a moment before dissolved into a singularly disarming smile. 'You have worked hard recently, Miss King. It has not gone unnoticed. When you go to Yorkshire for your sister's wedding then you must take more than just a few days off. Look on it as a holiday.'

'Yes. I'll try,' she said, more concerned about the time she was to spend at Stanfield during Maxine's absence than she was about her sister's wedding. She was not at all sure how she was going to survive two or three weeks alone with him without weakening her resolve to keep their relationship as a working one. 'Goodnight, Captain Frankland.'

As he watched her climb the stairs to her room, there was a determined predatory gleam in Alex's eye. Miss King might wish to appear supremely indifferent to him, but there was an irresistible element of sexual attraction between them that could not be denied forever. He had been honest when he had told her she intrigued and fascinated him, for she was beginning to affect him in a way no other woman had, to stimulate him in a way he had not experienced since before his tragic marriage to Pamela.

He was the one who had suggested to Maxine that a short holiday away from Stanfield would be good for her, but it had not been a ruse to get Cordelia alone. However, he found the prospect immensely appealing and his lips curved in a crooked, satisfied smile. Perhaps before Maxine returned he might be successful in getting Cordelia to drop her guard.

Chapter Five

The following day Cordelia went up to the attics to sort out some of the furniture left up there that was to be sold. Much of it was similar to her own family's furniture at Edenthorpe: hideous pieces of Jacobean and Elizabethan oak, bulbous and uncomfortable.

However, lifting up a pile of chintz covers, she pulled out four slightly scratched chairs, recognising them by their shield-shaped open backs as Hepplewhite. She set them aside to be restored at some future date; in her opinion they were too beautiful and far too valuable to sell. There was also a lovely Regency settee. Although Cordelia was aware that it was not 'à la mode' to like anything of that period at this time, she could imagine just how the settee would look after an upholsterer had restored it, and she considered it worth preserving.

There was a rather elegant dressing-table in the corner, its drawers stuffed with papers from the office. Carefully removing the drawers, she emptied out the papers—mainly invoices going back to before the War. Quickly her eyes scanned the dusty sheets to make sure there was nothing of importance before placing them in a box to take downstairs. On Alex's say-so, they would be burned in the incinerator.

Replacing the drawers, she picked up a bundle of papers that had been lodged at the back of the dressing-table, but had fallen out onto the floor. Believing them to be of no importance, she picked them up and placed them in the box with all the other papers but, just as she was about to turn away and go on to the next piece of furniture, something about their appearance drew her eyes back to them.

There were about five sheets, all fastened together with a paper clip. Retrieving them from the box, she soon realised they were letters. Thinking nothing of it, she began idly reading them, soon realising, as she deciphered the writing that sprawled across the pages, that she had stumbled upon something highly personal.

They were letters, love letters, addressed to Pamela Frankland, Alex's deceased wife. The dressing-table must have been Pamela's; she must have put them to the back of the drawers out of the way of prying eyes. Either that or they had become lodged there by accident.

Without realising that she was doing so, Cordelia held her breath as she turned the first of the letters over to read the signature at the end, for she knew the writing was not Alex's. It was signed: To my darling Pamela, with all my love, your adoring Michael.

Reluctant to read any more, for it was not in her nature to pry, Cordelia folded the letters and stared in front of her, wondering what she ought to do with them. Their contents suggested that Alex's wife had been having an affair while he was in France. If he had found out about this, then that would explain why no one ever spoke of her.

She did think it might be best for all concerned if she destroyed the letters, to pretend they had never existed, but she had no authority to do that and nor could she give them to Alex. She had no wish to cause him any unnecessary grief, for there was every possibility he had known nothing about his wife's infidelity. She would give them to Maxine, who would know what should be done with them. Tucking the letters into her pocket, Cordelia went outside to the gardens where she knew she could be found.

Maxine was a keen gardener, often to be found helping the head gardener in the greenhouses where beautiful carnations, orchids and exotic house plants were grown. The greenhouses were on the edge of the kitchen gardens that provided all the vegetables for the house as well as delicious peaches and nectarines and grapes in the vineries. Camellia trees grew against a huge brick wall that surrounded the kitchen gardens. When they were in bloom, the various coloured flowers were so profuse there was scarcely a gap between them.

Cordelia found Maxine in one of the potting sheds, a green baize apron covering the blue silk dress and a heap of sand loam and leaf mould on the table in front of her as she potted up seedlings and plants, wearing gloves to protect her hands.

She smiled brightly when Cordelia appeared in the doorway. 'Hello, Delia. What brings you down here? Fancy a bit of potting yourself?'

'No. I'll leave that to you experts,' she replied, thinking that behind her usual cheerful and bright façade, which she tried to maintain at all times, Maxine was showing signs of strain. Alex was right. Some time spent away from Stanfield Hall with her friends in Eastbourne, and the sea air, would be good for her.

Maxine paused, realising Cordelia was not her usual self. There was a troubled look in her eyes. 'Why—what's the matter, my dear? You look quite pale. Is there something wrong?'

'Yes—I mean—I'm not sure.' Sighing deeply, she moved closer to the older woman, glancing quickly around to make quite sure there was no one else in the potting shed to overhear.

'I've been up in the attics trying to sort out some of the furniture Captain Frankland intends selling. I—I came across a dressing-table—its drawers full of papers. When I removed them I—I came across some letters.' She took them from her pocket and handed them to Maxine. 'At first I didn't know what to do with them, but after careful consideration I thought it best that I give them to you.'

Laying down her trowel and removing her gloves, then wiping her hands down her apron, Maxine slowly reached out and took them from her, opening them with care, as if she already knew what they contained. After reading the first few lines she stopped, screwing her eyes up in horror and pain—as though she could not go on. Then she looked at Cordelia in devastating sorrow, seeming to age ten years before her eyes, her lips clamped together as she tried to bring herself under control.

'You know what these are? You have read them?'

'No, Maxine, not all of them,' Cordelia replied gently, her eyes filled with compassion. 'Just enough to know that I could not give them to Captain Frankland.'

'Thank you for that. To have done so would have revived so many ugly and bitter memories—memories best left in the past. Nothing would be gained by that. I would prefer it if he never finds out about these letters, Delia—that we keep this matter to ourselves. You do understand, don't you?'

'Yes. That is why I gave them to you.'

Maxine sighed, removing her apron and placing it on the table. 'I think I'll go on up to the house. Please excuse me, my dear. This has all come as something of a shock.'

Cordelia watched her go, her usually straight figure slightly stooped. She was about to follow her when suddenly a shadow fell across her path. Turning quickly, she found Alex beside her. For a moment she was so surprised to see him standing there that she felt as if all the breath had left her body and she could do nothing but stare up at him, wondering how long he had been there—how much he had heard.

'I apologise for startling you,' he said quietly. 'I was just coming to find you when I saw you talking to Maxine.' His eyes moved to Maxine's retreating figure and he frowned. 'Is she all right?'

'Yes—yes, of course,' said Cordelia hurriedly, hoping he was unable to detect that anything was amiss. 'I—I think she is needed back at the house. Why were you looking for me?'

'To ask if you would like to come riding with me. Some hunters I bought have arrived from Ireland and one, I think, will suit you well.'

Again he glanced towards where Maxine was climbing the steps of the terrace that led to the house, which gave Cordelia a moment to look at him admiringly. He was dressed for riding, looking stunning in camel breeches and glossy black riding boots and a black tight-fitting jacket, tall and perfectly proportioned with his broad shoulders and narrow, muscular hips.

Seeming to sense her eyes on him and the effect he was having on her, he looked down at her with his wicked, dangerously infuriating gaze, smiling slowly.

'Well? What do you say?'

'Yes—I'd like to. I'll go and change—if you don't mind waiting a few minutes?'

'No. I'll meet you at the stables.'

When Cordelia walked across the sunny stable yard, tall and elegant in her riding skirt and black brimmed hat, from which a veil of tantalising net was suspended over her face, Alex's look was one of appraisal.

Observing the stable lad just finishing fastening the fine leather side-saddle onto a gleaming chestnut mare, which Cordelia knew must be her mount, she thought it a pity that a lack of formality in these postwar years did not extend to the hunting field. At Edenthorpe she often rode astride, which she found much more natural and comfortable, but as yet ladies were not seen to ride that way in public.

Alex moved towards the horse, running his practised hands slowly over its quivering flanks. 'I particularly selected this mare. She's a good, gentle horse, one I'm sure will do well on the hunting field.'

'Not too gentle, I hope,' said Cordelia, looking up at him sideways whilst pulling on her gloves.

Alex helped her into the lady's saddle, sensing, as she slipped her booted feet into the stirrups and arranged her riding skirt, holding her whip skilfully, that she was no stranger to riding.

As they cantered out of the stable yard and galloped over the flat Norfolk landscape and he saw how effortlessly she cleared low hedges and fences, he began wishing he'd found her a more spirited mount to ride, one which would have been more in keeping with her character.

Coming to a village, Alex slowed his horse to a trot.

'I think we'll stop at the Black Swan on the main street for a drink before riding back. Would you like that?'

Cordelia had no objections to this; in fact, she would welcome a drink. The ride had made her thirsty.

Sliding off his huge black gelding in the inn yard, Alex walked towards Cordelia, intending to help her dismount, but she slipped out of the saddle and jumped to the ground with ease, denying him the pleasure of placing his hands on her slim waist and being close to her. When he observed her knowing narrowed look and the mischievous smile playing on her soft lips, he suspected she had sensed this and had purposely jumped down before he could reach her. The thought made him smile.

Rather than go inside the dim interior of the public house they chose to sit instead on some benches outside, attracting glances from passers-by, some doffing their hats in polite respect when they recognised Captain Frankland. Cordelia attracted some curious stares as people tried to work out who she was, not having seen her before; it was not often she strayed beyond the high walls of Stanfield Hall.

The landlord immediately came out to take their order, beaming broadly when he saw the identity of his customer, for it was always a privilege to serve Captain Frankland.

When the landlord had disappeared to fetch their lemonade and beer, Alex looked across at Cordelia, who sat flushed and relaxed on the bench across the small table which separated them.

'How do you feel now?' he asked.

'Wonderful,' she laughed, her eyes shining. 'It's been so long since I've ridden that I'd almost forgotten what an invigorating experience it always is.'

'I'm impressed. You ride extremely well, Miss King—as well, if not better, than any woman I know. You must take part in the next hunt meet, which I intend to host at Stanfield.'

'I'd love to. When will that be?'

'Some time during August or September. It will be the first to be held at Stanfield since the outbreak of the War. Hunting was the main thing in those days—starting in the middle of August and going right through until May.'

Cordelia almost found herself saying how it had been the same at Edenthorpe but caught herself in time.

'Like my father and grandfather, I was born and bred in the hunting field but now,' Alex went on somewhat sadly, 'I have to say that I feel reluctant to ride to hounds after the blood of war.'

'I can understand that,' said Cordelia quietly. 'Do you intend buying more horses?'

'Yes. Unfortunately, it's an expensive business.'

'Buy more racehorses and you might get a return for your money when you eventually race them.'

'Hopefully—if they turn out to be any good. Before the War I was interested in breeding hunters, which I sold to the army for the purpose of remounts. But since the War the bloodstock industry—from a racing point of view—is expanding, so I wouldn't mind buying more racehorses. I'd very much like to get hold of one to train—to make it into a racehorse—seeing it improve.'

Cordelia laughed lightly. 'If you want to go

through the emotional and financial mill of buying and training highly bred horses for the sake of winning—for a slice of glory, so to speak—then I wish you luck, but I suspect it is a perilous gamble—one that could become a dangerous obsession.'

'I am too level-headed for that. But you speak as if you know what life is like in the winners' enclosure, Miss King. Do you?'

'No—of course not. But I can well imagine. I only hope your dream of being a top-class race-horse owner does not end up as a nightmare.'

Cordelia took a sip of the lemonade the land-lord had brought her, thinking how similar Alex's upbringing at Stanfield must have been to her own at Edenthorpe—and especially to that of her brothers. For years their lives had revolved around the stables, the hounds and the hunt.

'Tell me about yourself, Miss King, and where you learned to ride so superbly.'

Cordelia took another sip of her lemonade while she thought over his question—of how she could answer it without having to declare that her father was a peer of the realm. Sitting across from him, she was unable to avoid meeting those pen-etrating grey eyes, and each time he smiled she was already too well aware of the effect the beguiling quality of that smile was having on her.

'I learned to ride at home,' she said truthfully. 'My brothers and sisters—we all did.'

'I see. And did your father own the horses you rode?'

'Yes. A few.' She replaced her glass on the table in front of her, rather nervously, for she did not like the way the conversation had switched to herself. 'But nothing as grand as what you have at Stanfield.' This was not quite true; her father had some of the finest stables in Yorkshire, but Alex need not know that.

'I suspect you are being too modest, Miss King.' He spoke slowly, giving her a long, languorous look. 'What is your father's occupation?'

'I told you. He is a businessman—and if you don't mind I would rather not discuss it.'

Alex's expression did not change. 'Very well, we will not discuss it. But I am convinced you are not what you would like me to think you are.'

'Oh? Then what am I?' she teased.

'A very attractive young lady who, for some inexplicable reason, chooses to remain a mystery. But I will lay a wager that you are not the daughter of a poor man.'

'How very sceptical of you, but I only lay wagers on horses, Captain Frankland, and, as you already know, I have a habit of winning. Which reminds me—I've been meaning to ask you, what did you put your money on for the Gold Cup at Ascot?'

Again he smiled, mildly cynical, his finger slowly caressing the rim of his glass in a rather lascivious way as he continued to watch her closely. 'Let us say that, after taking note of some inside information on the course—from a lady who will remain nameless, but who takes an avid interest in racing—I backed the winner.'

Fully aware that she was the lady he spoke of, Cordelia's mouth widened in a smile and she could not resist saying smugly, 'So—you did back Periosteum after all.'

Her smile was infectious, causing Alex to smile broadly, his white teeth strong and gleaming in his tanned face. 'And did very nicely out of it, too. In fact, I must remember to ask the lady to accompany me to the next race meeting I attend, for—who knows? If I listen closely to her advice, then I may amass enough wealth to enable me to finance my entire stables.'

'I very much doubt it,' she laughed, rising and pulling on her gloves as they prepared to leave, 'for if the lady you speak of is as astute as you say she is, then she would be running a racing stable of her own.'

'And very successfully too, I am certain.'

Exchanging smiles they mounted and rode back to Stanfield Hall in a relaxed mood, any constraint between them having vanished for the time being.

The day Maxine left for Eastbourne was hot, like all the ones preceding it that summer. When Cordelia came out of the house to stand on the terrace overlooking the garden, the sun was beginning to go down in glowing lines of crimson, like ribbons flung across a sky the colour of indigo, radiant in its clarity. She was engulfed in a dull kind of lethargy, breathing in the warm, sweet scented air, enjoying the coolness that came with evening after the sweltering heat of the day.

Everything around her was peaceful and silent, the workmen having finished their work on the house long since and most of the servants having left for their homes in the nearby village. The birds were now silent and there was not even a breeze to stir the occasional leaf and fallen rose petals that littered the surface of the lawn.

She sighed, looking up at the glow of the setting sun glancing off the orange- and yellow-tinted tips of the leaves on the upper branches of the trees in the garden, feeling a peace and contentment wash over her—like a whisper, an excited expectancy, of things to come.

She smiled for no reason, wondering if this sudden feeling of elation and happiness warming her heart had been brought about by the knowledge that she was to spend some time alone with Alex during Maxine's absence. Oh, there would be the usual clamour of workmen and the bustle of servants around the house during the day, but the time would come, like now, when they would have gone and she would be alone with Alex.

It was against her better judgement that she allowed her thoughts to wander idly along these lines—until she heard the sound of a car approaching the front of the house, its wheels crunching the gravel on the driveway. Instinctively she knew it would be Alex, returning from taking Maxine to the station.

After a while there was a light tread behind her on the terrace but she didn't turn, knowing it couldn't be anyone else other than Alex.

'Did Maxine get off all right?' she enquired.

'Yes,' he replied softly, coming to stand close beside her, observing her look of preoccupation and falling in with her mood. 'What are you thinking?' he asked, his voice very low and quiet.

'Oh,' she sighed, thinking how wonderfully attractive he looked with his hair neatly brushed back, 'just how peaceful everything is—and how lovely the garden always looks at this time of day.'

Alex smiled, the guilty, self-satisfied smile of a conspirator, hoping the peace and intimacy of this moment was a foretaste of the time they would spend together while Maxine was away.

'Although I must say,' Cordelia said, smiling up at him, 'that if we have many more days as hot as today has been, then I shall begin to envy Maxine being beside the sea at Eastbourne with those wonderful, cooling sea breezes.'

'You do have a point.'

'Who is she staying with?'

'Friends of long standing. She doesn't often get to see them, unfortunately. She dedicated herself to the hospital here at Stanfield throughout the War, leaving herself little time for socialising and visiting friends.'

'Has she no family?'

'No—no one close—apart from myself, that is. I've always been extremely fond of her. When her husband died, followed so soon by my mother just before the War, it suited us both that she come to live at Stanfield. In fact, I don't know how I would have survived without her. She's a remarkable woman.'

At that moment Cook came out onto the terrace to ask Cordelia if she would like her evening meal sent up to her room.

Before she could tell her to do just that, Alex answered quickly, 'Miss King will be dining with me this evening, Mrs Morton—and every evening my aunt is in Eastbourne. Have another place set at the dining table, will you?'

With a little, knowing smile Mrs Morton went to do his bidding and Alex disappeared into the house, reappearing a moment later with two glasses of wine, handing one to Cordelia who gave him a questioning look.

'I hope you don't mind—but with Maxine away you don't expect me to dine alone, do you, Miss King?'

Cordelia didn't answer him, for as he handed her the glass of wine their fingers brushed together and she realised how close he was to her, smiling into her eyes with that slightly mocking, secretive smile of his.

Each of them was becoming aware of the strong, intensity of feeling developing between them and Cordelia was filled with a sudden glow not unknown to her, which she often experienced when she was with him, making her long for him to be closer still. She took a sip of her wine, lowering her eyes lest they revealed too much.

'Are you hungry?' he asked.

'A little,' she answered, her voice a little uncertain, for she realised that, however determined she was to keep their relationship strictly platonic, it was going to be extremely difficult if they were to share an intimate dinner each evening.

But no matter what romantic thoughts Cordelia nurtured concerning Alex and herself, she told herself that she must not bow to them. Alex was very much aware of her as a woman—this she knew by the sensuous manner in which he regarded her, and on occasion by the very tone of his voice when he spoke to her and the look in his eyes. Being with him day after day, she knew she was in danger of falling hopelessly under his spell, but whatever happened she must not give way to recklessness with him.

She would have to be careful; she could not afford to become involved with him in any way other than work. He was her employer; if she wanted to retain her sanity and her job, then that was how it must remain, for she had worked too hard to achieve her independence to allow it to be encumbered by a love affair—however appealing she felt this to be. If there was any danger that she might become overwhelmed by him, she would have no choice but to seek employment elsewhere.

Chapter Six

As the days spilled into one another, their time was well occupied with estate matters and instructing the workmen, who had almost finished the repairs and renovations to the Hall. They also visited several horse sales up and down the country, and Alex presided over some meetings with his tenant farmers, discussing at length new methods of farming which could be introduced to make the estate more profitable in these postwar days of high taxation.

That day had been a particularly long and tiring one. From his room, Alex watched Cordelia where she walked in the garden below. She moved languidly along the paths, having changed for the evening into a sheath-like lemon silk dress.

He watched her in fascination, savouring the different tones of colour playing on the bare flesh of her shoulders and arms. Her golden head was uncovered and shone in the light and shade beneath the rich foliage of the trees. The sun was down now and a luminous haze had begun to settle on the garden, lengthening the shadows of the trees.

Alex was deeply troubled as he watched her, for the fact that he was beginning to see her more and more as an extremely desirable woman—a woman he believed he was falling in love with—was beginning to outweigh her secretarial skills. Surprisingly there had been no joy in this discovery and, with hindsight, he now knew it was a situation he should have tried to avoid.

That she shared his own feelings he knew without being told, but these feelings must be suppressed for the time being. As long as she continued to think of him as her employer, with nothing between them to threaten her single-minded independence, which was so important to her, then matters would continue very much the same. But should their relationship change to anything deeper, then there was a strong possibility that he would lose her altogether. They stood on the brink of passion, neither of them daring to overstep the mark.

It had not escaped his notice that she had been quiet and preoccupied all that day, which they had spent at Newmarket. She had certainly not been herself. Something was clearly troubling her, but what it could be he had no idea. Perhaps it had something to do with her work? If this was the case, then maybe he was in a position to put it right. With an air of determination he went down to the garden.

Cordelia started when she found Alex standing beside her, not having seen or heard him approach. She looked up at him, her eyes dark and velvety in a creamy pale face. He was disturbed for she gave him a look of absorbed concentration that seemed to come from deep and far, or from a memory with which she struggled that was too painful for her to remember. He thought she must be either unwell or suffering from some deep sorrow.

Alex was justified in his concern, for that morning Cordelia had awoken with a heavy feeling of sadness. Today had been like a piece of memory come back—it would have been her brother Billy's birthday. She couldn't help reliving in her mind that day before the War when Billy had been fifteen and they had celebrated his birthday at Edenthorpe, all the more poignant because her own twelfth birthday had followed two days later. They were the last birthdays they had shared together.

Through that day with Alex she had hoped her work would take her mind off Billy, but it hadn't. He had been everywhere—in the cadence of a voice of a passer-by in the street, his likeness in the face of a stranger on the next table in the restaurant where she had shared a meal with Alex. She had not been able to dispel his image from her mind.

She raised her eyes and there was a sad, brooding look in them. Alex was struck by the mournful look on her face.

'Forgive me, Miss King, if I intrude, but I cannot help observing that you have not been your normal, cheerful self today. You have been far away. If you are unwell—or if there is something troubling you and you would like a sympathetic ear—then I am at your disposal.'

His seriousness brought a smile to Cordelia's lips. 'It is nothing to be concerned about, I assure you—and I am quite well,' she sighed. 'It's just memories—that's all. I—I was thinking about my brother, you see. He was killed in the War.'

With deep understanding Alex nodded gravely. 'I see. I'm sorry. It is natural that you should mourn him.'

'It is just that—well—today would have been his birthday.'

Cordelia could feel her eyes filling with tears and she turned away quickly, ashamed of herself for showing her emotions. With an effort Alex restrained himself from moving closer.

'I'm sorry,' Cordelia went on. 'Nothing will ever bring him back—I know, it's just that his birthday always brings back such poignant memories. He's been dead four years now and you'd think I would have got used to not having him around. But it's not that simple when you have been close to someone all your life. Usually I'm all right but—well—it's just on days like today—his birthday. Do you understand what I mean?'

'Yes, I do,' he answered, beginning to feel a trifle envious of the deceased Billy for being able to evoke such devotion after all these years.

'He—he was engaged to be married to a lovely girl. Their future together looked so bright.'

'The trouble with life, Miss King, is that it is never what we expect—and in many cases that could be a blessing.'

Cordelia looked at him curiously for there was a deep poignancy to his voice. She would have liked to have asked him what he meant by that but thought better of it. No one would ever know the emptiness Billy's death had brought to her life, but Alex seemed to sense it.

'When you lose someone close—in war or in peace—you have to carry on, however painful that is at first. It is something you have to do,' Alex went on in a quiet voice. 'You have to get on with it. You and your brother must have been very close.'

'Yes—we were. I have another brother much older but Billy was just three years and two days older than I. Before the War—it was the last time we celebrated our birthdays together. Billy was fifteen and I was twelve. We had a party at home. I'll never forget it.'

'Your family must have been a consolation to you when he died.'

'No. Oddly enough, they seemed to clam up after his death. No one wanted to talk about it.'

'But you did?'

'Yes. Very much.'

Alex sighed. 'The War claimed many lives—English, French and German. Few families remained untouched by it.'

Cordelia looked at him suddenly, remembering that he too had a loss to bear.

'Oh—how thoughtless of me. Maxine told me you lost your wife in an air raid,' she said quietly.

Alex didn't reply. His grey eyes darkened, but not with sadness. It was then Cordelia thought of the letters which she had been unable to banish from her mind. Maxine had told her nothing to appease her curiosity—in fact, her reaction at the time had only succeeded in increasing it.

Looking across at Alex, she saw nothing to indicate the pain his wife's infidelity and death must have caused him, and once again she wondered if he had been aware of it. She suddenly felt awkward, wishing she hadn't brought the subject of his wife up.

'I'm sorry. I shouldn't have mentioned it,' she said. 'It must be very painful for you.'

Alex frowned and there was a hard glint in his eyes. 'Yes—something like that.'

'You—you were injured in the War,' Cordelia said in an attempt to steer the conversation away from his wife. 'Did you return to your regiment afterwards?'

'Why not? It was never a handicap. Apart from a slight limp, it gives me little trouble. At which battle was your brother killed?'

'The third battle of Ypres—or Passchendaele—the third battle of the mud I believe Lloyd George called it.'

'I know. It was there I was wounded.'

'What was it like?'

Alex looked down at her, his expression dark and serious in the gathering dusk. 'Are you sure you want me to tell you?'

'Yes. I know so little. David—my older brother—he was there but has always refused to speak of it, so please tell me truthfully.'

'Very well.' His eyes became hard with unforgettable memories when they became fixed on hers. 'It was hell—as I remember. The struggle went on for three months. Everything went wrong that could go wrong. The drainage system of Flanders broke down—and, to make matters worse, it was the wettest August for many years.

'The tanks, which had become a practical instrument of war, could not be used—the guns sank and men struggled forward up to their waists in mud. The tragic irony of it all was, when it was over, the British had advanced no more than four miles. Passchendaele did little to improve the morale of the British army.'

'I can see that,' whispered Cordelia, engulfed with a deep sadness when she thought what her brother and thousands of other soldiers had been forced to endure. 'It must have been dreadful. Poor Billy.'

Alex saw her lips tremble and she put up her fingers to still them, turning away. His eyes travelled admiringly over her gracefully bowed head and, studying the pure line of her profile in the dwindling light, his fingers touched her arm lightly.

She turned back to him, composed now. His gaze was compelling and Cordelia knew, by some miraculous communication from his mesmeric grey eyes, that he was thinking of the moment he had touched her arm. Neither of them spoke but something passed between them that they both fully understood.

Cordelia lowered her gaze and Alex looked away, deeply aware that if they remained in the garden much longer, cloaked in the secret intimacy of the trees, he was very much in danger of overstepping the invisible barrier she had built between them and taking her in his arms.

'Come,' he said, not wishing to disturb the harmony which had sprung up between them, and yet at the same time not wishing to embarrass her by creating a situation they might both regret later—one which could have a disastrous effect on their employer—employee relationship, 'it's getting dark. We'll go back inside and have a brandy. I think you could do with one.

'I realise I might have been working you too hard whilst Maxine has been away—giving you little time to relax. So, if you feel like taking tomorrow off, I won't mind.'

Cordelia looked up at him, noticing that his dark hair had been brushed smoothly back from his forehead and gleamed in the orange glow shining from the windows of the house. His lips were curved in a smile. Something which she was beginning to recognise but was too afraid to analyse, knowing it would be sure to lead to complications between them, stirred within her heart.

'No. I wouldn't dream of it. Besides,' she said on a lighter note, falling into step beside him as they went back into the house, her mind dwelling with wonder on the compassion she had seen in his eyes, his voice devoid of any mockery, and the consolation his nearness had brought her, 'tomorrow there is much to do—with that little filly you bought today at Newmarket being delivered.

'Not only that,' she said, her voice reduced to almost a whisper, as if speaking to herself, 'I would probably feel much worse if I were alone.'

* * *

Two days later Cordelia went downstairs, fully expecting to spend a busy day in the office—but, on meeting Alex in the hall, she soon realised he had other ideas. He was casually dressed in a pale blue shirt and light grey trousers, which only served to set off his dazzling good looks. His sleek black hair still looked slightly damp from his bath and she caught the scent of pine shaving lotion, which she would always associate with him.

He was completely relaxed, his smile creasing the corners of his grey eyes and softening his slightly arrogant features.

'Today we are not working, Miss King. I think we have both earned some time off for relaxation, don't you? I'm sure you will be pleased to learn there is not a horse sale or a balance sheet on the itinerary.'

Cordelia stared at him in astonishment. 'Then what have you in mind?'

'I thought we might take a drive into Cambridge—the city of my youth, I might add, for I was a student there. We will explore the old streets—shop if the fancy takes us—and stroll by the River Cam. Mrs Morton is to prepare a picnic basket for us. Does that appeal to you?'

At first Cordelia hesitated at the thought of spending the whole day alone with him, without the protective shell her position as his secretary always gave her, but her hesitation only lasted a moment. She could not deny that she was tired and it would be nice to relax for a while. A drive along the leafy lanes to Cambridge would make a pleasant change.

'Yes—it does sound very appealing,' she smiled. 'I'll go and change.'

'Then I'll meet you in the dining-room, and after breakfast we'll make a start.'

The day was hot, the sun shining down out of a clear blue sky as they drove the thirty miles or so towards Cambridge. The narrow, enchanting lanes meandered through a peaceful landscape of broad fields, orchards and delightful, slumbering villages; the skyline interrupted by an occasional windmill and church tower; the flat stretches of the fens interspaced with ditches, mostly dry after the unusually long hot summer.

As Cordelia relaxed against the leather upholstery of Alex's Daimler, she sighed with deep contentment. It was to be a day of discovery and unforgettable wonder.

On reaching the ancient university city, where Alex had been an undergraduate at St John's College before the War, he immediately insisted on giving her a grand tour of the superb buildings and their many courts, then crossing over the beautiful Bridge of Sighs spanning the River Cam, where peaceful lawns and meadows sloped down to the water's edge, before exploring the city's delightful collection of old streets, and idly browsing in the shops.

Cordelia bought several items, but resisted the temptation to purchase a small gold crucifix on a gold chain in a jeweller's shop, for if Alex saw her buying something so expensive he would no doubt make some flippant remark about her grandmother's legacy being inexhaustible.

They picnicked along the grassy banks of the willow-lined river, slowly eating the delicious food Mrs Morton had packed for them, which was more like a feast, the chicken and ham, cheese and fresh fruit washed down with a delicious white wine.

The day passed in a wondrous warm haze. They discussed many things; in fact, they had never talked so much. The conversation stimulated Cordelia's imagination; she was excited by it.

Alex's lean body was stretched lazily out on the grass. He looked across to where Cordelia sat, completely at her ease, her face slightly pink from the effects of the wine and having caught the sun. They talked and were silent, comfortable to be in each other's company, content to sit in the shade of the willow and watch the students lazily punting on the river.

'Are you enjoying today?' Alex asked.

She sighed. 'Very much. I envy you being a student here. It's a beautiful city.'

'Then you'll have to come again.'

'Yes, I will,' she replied, admiring his clean-cut profile and strong body as he leaned across to fill her glass, even though it was still half-full. The hot summer sun had turned his skin a wonderful shade of olive. He caught her eye and found her studying him. She flushed and he smiled.

'What time do we have to leave?' she asked, vulnerable suddenly, taking another sip of her wine in an attempt to hide the confusion he was beginning to cause to her emotions, wishing they didn't have to return to Stanfield at all.

'Oh—not yet. There's no hurry.' He was silent for a moment, studying her, before he next spoke. 'You haven't been to London since Maxine went to Eastbourne. Will you be going this weekend?'

'No, I shouldn't think so. Why do you ask?'

'No reason,' he said absently. 'I thought perhaps you might be eager to get back to your young man.'

'What young man?'

'The one you were with at Ascot.'

'Jeremy! He isn't my young man,' she said with some asperity. 'He's an acquaintance, that's all. He just happened to be my escort for the day at Ascot.'

Relieved that this was all the high-spirited young man was to her, Alex nodded slightly. 'I see.' He sighed deeply, wistfully, noticing the slight curve of her breast beneath the white linen of her dress, wanting to reach out and touch her fingers which were curled round the stem of her glass.

They continued to talk at leisure, Alex telling her what it had been like to be a student at Cambridge, and Cordelia was content to listen, basking in his sharing of all he knew about this ancient city of learning beneath its noble spires.

It was with reluctance that they left it behind, returning to Stanfield where Cordelia luxuriated in a warm scented bath, deliciously weary after an enchanting day.

But the day was far from over. They dined alone, chatting about inconsequential things, content to be in each other's company. They ate and sipped their wine, afterwards taking a stroll in the garden, and anyone seeing them together would believe they were lovers.

As the calm of the evening drew to a close Alex escorted Cordelia up the stairs to her room, pausing for a moment before her door and handing her a black, narrow leather box. She looked at him, slightly bemused, before opening it to see the gold crucifix she had so admired earlier that day in the jeweller's shop in Cambridge. She lifted her eyes and stared at him.

'I—I cannot accept this.'

'Of course you can. I saw how much you admired it.'

'But—but why are you giving me this?'

His eyes twinkled wickedly. 'It is your birthday, isn't it?'

Cordelia stared at him in disbelief. 'But—how did you know?'

'You told me. Two days after your brother, if I remember correctly. One doesn't have to be a genius to work it out.'

'Nevertheless—you must see why I cannot accept it.'

'If you won't accept it as a gift from me to you for your birthday—then please accept it as a token of my thanks and appreciation for all the hard work you have done for me. Besides, you gave me the pleasure of your company today, which I have enjoyed immensely. Do not deny me the pleasure of giving you something in return.'

Cordelia smiled, looking once again at the crucifix glowing warmly on its bed of soft purple velvet.

'You are extremely persuasive.'

'I know. Does that mean you'll accept it?'

'Yes,' she said softly, looking into his eyes and knowing he would be hurt if she refused. 'How can I refuse? Thank you.'

'It's my pleasure. Now—open the door. There should be another surprise waiting for you—if Mrs Morton has done as I instructed.'

Totally bewildered, Cordelia pushed open the door, completely dumbfounded on finding her room filled with vases of all kinds of exotic flowers, their scents quite intoxicating.

'Oh,' she gasped in wonderment, 'they're beautiful.'

Alex smiled, pleased with her reaction. She turned to him in astonishment.

'Happy birthday, Miss King,' he said, unable to resist bending his head and placing his lips lightly on her cheek. At first she resisted, but then, as she was about to offer him her lips, he drew away. Smiling a wonderfully engaging smile, he left her standing there, closing the door softly behind him.

That was the moment when Cordelia realised she was in love with him.

Totally bemused, Cordelia sat on her bed, staring at the beautiful array of flowers, thinking over the events of the day and Alex's surprising behaviour. He had been an attentive, polite, considerate companion and had made no advances towards her. They had been relaxed in each other's company, but she had not been immune to the sensuality he was holding in tight control behind his careful reserve.

She admired his restraint, but how much longer was she going to be able to deny the strong physical attraction growing between them? Especially after his generous gift and the flowers—and then his parting kiss. Lightly she touched her cheek, where his lips had lingered, and sighed. It would be better when Maxine returned and they were not together quite so much. But, in the meantime, how was she to deal with this new problem that had presented itself?

Feeling restless and unable to sleep she took another bath, soaking for a long time in the lavender-scented water, feeling her body beginning to relax. The bath helped to soothe her, but she could not dispel Alex from her thoughts. What would she do if he attempted to change the situation between them?

He believed her to be an ordinary working woman and men of his status did not marry that kind of woman. They married women like Diana Hibbert—or herself, Cordelia Hamilton-King, as she had been before she had chosen to conceal her true identity.

But she did not want to be married. She had gone to too much trouble to achieve her independence to throw it all away when the first man came along who attracted her.

But she loved Alex Frankland, so nothing was going to be simple while she remained in his employ—and now it would be twice as hard for her to leave. If her independence did not mean so much to her, then the barriers that separated them were not too formidable for them to surmount, but would he ever forgive her deception for pretending to be someone else?

* * *

The following morning Cordelia went down to breakfast, determined to put the previous day behind her and think of it as nothing more than a pleasant memory—until she saw Alex and almost weakened. But he greeted her as he did every morning, with a polite reserve. Clearly it was business as usual and, even though Cordelia was slightly hurt and offended by this, deep down she was grateful to him, for it would make her own resolution not to succumb to her emotions that much easier.

Chapter Seven

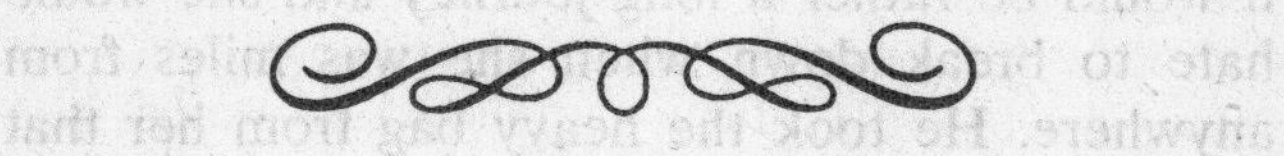

Autumn was upon them when Maxine returned to Stanfield Hall in good spirits. It was clear that the holiday she had spent with her friends in Eastbourne had done her good. However, she had no sooner arrived back than Cordelia had to leave for Edenthorpe for her sister's wedding.

Her feelings towards Alex were complex; in fact, the more she was with him the deeper her love seemed to grow. But the force of attraction he aroused in her worried her, for she imagined that, if she did not do something about it, he would overturn her life.

Ever since he had returned to Stanfield—when Cordelia had first discovered he was her employer—hardly a day had gone by when they had not been together, and now the time had come for them to part—only for a week, yet it was a terrible wrench. But she had to get away to put her thoughts in order—which she could not do while she was distracted by his presence at Stanfield. Emily's wedding provided the excuse she needed to be by herself for a while—to sort out the muddle she found herself to be in.

Alex was to run her to the station—she would have liked to drive herself up to Edenthorpe, but it would be rather a long journey and she would hate to break down when she was miles from anywhere. He took the heavy bag from her that she was struggling with, placing it in the boot with comparative ease.

'Thank you. It is rather heavy,' she said, trying not to think of how handsome he looked with his sleek black hair combed back, his tanned skin stretched tight over his cheekbones and his grey eyes expressionless.

'So it is. Anyone would think you weren't coming back,' he said with an ironic glint in his eyes, thinking how fetching she looked in her pale peach-coloured jumper suit and matching hat. 'There will be someone to meet you when you get to Leeds?'

'Yes,' she replied, ignoring his remark about not coming back. 'My father will be at the station.'

'You are looking forward to going home?' he asked as the car sped down the drive.

'Yes. It's been a long time since I saw my family.'

'Make the most of it. You've earned some time

off. I can well imagine that when you first came to Stanfield the workload must have seemed Herculean, but the way you plunged in with such tremendous enthusiasm, delegating certain household tasks among the servants, reserving for yourself the mountain of paperwork in the office, and the accounts concerning both household and estate affairs, has been exemplary.'

'I cannot take the credit for doing it all. Maxine has done more than her share. She is a remarkable woman.'

'I know. However—I intend finding an agent to take over estate matters—as was the case in my father's time. That should ease your workload.' He suddenly looked at her thoughtfully. 'You did enjoy the day we spent in Cambridge, didn't you?'

'Yes—although I believe you know I did—especially the picnic beside the river,' she said softly, finding her eyes captured by his when she looked across at him, feeling herself flushing slightly, for it was the first time either of them had mentioned that day they had both enjoyed so much.

Alex stopped the car when they reached the end of the drive. Having to wait until the way was clear of traffic before he could pull out, he contemplated her for a moment. Cordelia was drawn by his gaze like a moth to a bright light. Mesmerised by the depths in her hazel eyes, by her lips slightly parted and moist, Alex had to master an urge almost beyond his control to reach out and take her in his arms.

With reluctance, Cordelia tore her eyes from his as he pulled out onto the main road.

'You will be back for the hunt?' said Alex.

'Yes. In good time.'

'I hope so. James is a man accustomed to the satisfaction of all his needs,' he said jokingly. 'He will be quite desolate if you're not here.'

'Oh—I dare say he'll get over it,' she replied coolly, having wondered when she was going to have the pleasure of meeting James Hibbert again and surprised she hadn't seen him again at Edenthorpe before now. 'You and James have been friends for a long time, haven't you?'

'We were at school together. He was a bit wild even then.' He gave Cordelia a look she couldn't quite fathom, examining her as though looking for some reaction, his voice much too casual when he spoke of James. 'Perhaps he's looking for someone to reform him.'

'Maybe he is. But I don't envy the woman who takes him on. He may be wealthy, but he is too good looking and too much of a playboy ever to remain faithful to one woman. Don't worry. I'll be back in plenty of time to help organise the hunt,' she replied, refusing to be drawn further on the subject of James Hibbert.

Alex glanced across at her before smiling slightly, seemingly satisfied with her reply. Happily she was too intelligent to be taken in by a charmer such as James. He'd hate to see her become entangled with a practised philanderer who had loved and left many a young woman nursing a broken heart. 'You will ride with us?'

'I'd love to because I do so love riding—even though I shall be hoping the fox outruns the hounds. It's hardly my idea of fun—or sport, for that matter, seeing a defenceless creature pulled apart by a pack of hounds.'

'You might change your mind if you were to see the interior of a chicken coop after a fox has had its way—or witnessed one taking a newborn lamb from its mother.'

'I have, several times, and I know they are a scourge to farmers, but I think there are kinder ways of disposing of the fox. Shooting it would be more humane.'

Alex smiled. 'Don't worry. If you were to see the sorry state of my unruly pack, then there is every possibility that the fox will end up chasing the hounds.'

When they reached the station, Alex insisted on escorting her onto the platform and waiting until the train had pulled in before leaving her. 'Goodbye, Miss King. Please take care—and take some extra days off if you wish—although I don't know how we'll manage without you,' he said with mock seriousness, but then he smiled. 'I trust all will go well with your sister's wedding. Give my regards to your family.'

He stood and watched the train disappear along the track before returning to Stanfield, which seemed strangely empty now she was no longer there.

Unbeknown to Alex as he drove Cordelia to the station, a curtain in one of the upstairs windows fell back into place as Maxine, who had watched them leave, stood back, her face etched with lines of concern. She wasn't blind and could see what was happening between her nephew and his secretary.

They were deeply attracted to each other and both were fighting to keep their emotions in check. Whenever they were together the air was charged with a vibrancy no one could fail to be aware of. As might be the case with many young ladies in Delia's position, Alex, with his wealth and good looks, would be considered a worthy catch indeed, but she knew Delia well enough to know she would consider such things immaterial.

The trouble was that Maxine had become extremely fond of her. She liked the way Cordelia had slipped in with the perfect ease of one born to life in a house like Stanfield, and that she had a strong sense of knowing how things should be done and an awareness and respect of the old traditions.

Maxine would be sorry to lose her, for she might take it into her head to leave Stanfield if she saw her relationship with her employer getting in the way of her career—which would be a great pity, for she and Alex were ideally suited for one another.

Edenthorpe was in a state of upheaval over Emily's forthcoming marriage to the son of a lord from the north of England, with great excitement throughout the house. When Cordelia arrived guests from all over the country were already beginning to fill the vacant rooms that had been got ready for the occasion.

Emily was in a panic that they weren't going to be ready on time but her mother, being her usual efficient and well-organised self, was adamant that nothing could possibly go wrong—with the exception of Cordelia's bridesmaid's dress, that is.

As Cordelia was the chief bridesmaid, her mother had ordered the dress to be made to her daughter's measurements in her absence—and she lost no time in letting her know it had been a nuisance and that she should have been at Edenthorpe, on hand for the seamstress and to help with the preparations for her sister's wedding.

It was no use Cordelia going over the old argument about her independence and wanting to make her own way in life, that now she had a responsible position she could not just come home whenever her mother ordered her to, so she just sighed submissively and said, 'Yes, Mother.'

Unlike Cordelia, who had battled to get her own way to win her freedom from the monotonous routine of upper-class family life, Emily was quite different. She was content with a quiet country life, passionately interested in horses and dogs, and was happy to help her mother with the local Conservative rallies and fund-raising garden fêtes.

Her marriage was the most spectacular society wedding Leeds had seen in a long time, covered by newspaper reporters and photographers alike, with crowds of excited people standing in the streets to watch the groom and then the bridesmaids arriving, followed by the radiant bride on the arm of her proud father.

Class distinctions of the old world, which were still considered to be the fundamental basis of society, had not as yet become a widespread subject for envy and hatred as they were later to become, so it was fun for ordinary people to stand and watch the aristocratic guests arriving in their shining cars with liveried chauffeurs and footmen in front.

Emily was calm—the perfect bride, her mother said, with meaningful emphasis in her look when her eyes fastened on Cordelia. After the ceremony, a splendid reception was held at

Edenthorpe. No expense had been spared on the food and Emily's elaborate trousseau.

After the endless speeches had been made and toasts to the happy couple drunk, the cake cut and the photographs taken and they had changed and left for their honeymoon in the south of France, the guests began to dwindle and once again the house slowly returned to normal.

To Cordelia, it was a relief now that it was all over and she had a couple of days to herself before she had to return to Stanfield Hall. There had been so much to do throughout the days preceding the wedding followed by the wedding day itself, that she'd purposely tried to thrust all thoughts of Alex from her mind, but now it was over he occupied her every waking moment.

Deep inside, she knew she would have to leave Stanfield Hall, painful as this would be for her, if she wanted to continue her career unencumbered by her emotions. But it was then that she discovered a weakness in herself, for how could she bear to leave Alex, loving him as she did? And yet, if she didn't leave soon she wasn't going to be able to. In a concerted effort to come to a decision, she decided to wait until after the hunt before she told him she would be leaving his employ.

Lord Langhorne could not believe that the young lady who sat so confidently across from him next to his wife at the dining-table, with her smooth golden head bowed over her plate, was his daughter. There was a look of determination about her and an obstinate air of resolve in the square set of her chin that had been absent before she had left Edenthorpe to forge a career for herself. She had a built-in awareness that was necessary if one wanted to succeed in the world of business.

But there was also something else. She had always been unable to hide from him, while she had been growing up, when something was troubling her—as it was now.

'The house will seem so empty now—with Emily gone,' said his wife.

Cordelia looked at her warily. 'You'll have Georgina and the children coming to stay, Mother, and David is often home.'

'Perhaps you could get home more often, dear. We see so little of you these days.'

'I promise I'll get home when I can.'

'You look tired, Cordelia,' her father said. 'Can't you take a few more days off from that job of yours?'

'No—unfortunately I can't.' She lowered her eyes, hating herself for lying to them. Hadn't Alex told her to take a few more days off if she wished, to look on it as a holiday? But the truth of the matter was that she was missing him dreadfully and couldn't wait to return to Stanfield.

'Well—I think you're working too hard,' her

mother remarked. 'Everyone has to take time off from work occasionally.'

'I don't work all the time, Mother. I often manage to get back to the flat in London at weekends.'

'Yes—and that's another thing I've been meaning to speak to you about.'

'Oh?'

'Is there any point in keeping that flat on any longer? Especially as you're living in at Stanfield Hall. You could just as easily come home to Edenthorpe when you have a weekend off.'

'But I want to keep the flat on, Mother. Besides, I do so love London—and I would miss not seeing Kitty.'

'Oh—very well,' sighed her mother, knowing Cordelia was not to be persuaded.'

'What's she like—this Lady McBride?' asked her father.

'Maxine? Oh, she's a pleasant, loveable person. I've been lucky having her to show me what has to be done. Although it's her nephew I work for. She merely interviewed me for the position as secretary in his absence.'

'And what sort of work do you do?' asked her mother. 'It's all so mysterious.'

'Not really,' said Cordelia, telling them all about Stanfield Hall, now it had been used for a convalescent hospital during the War and how it was now being restored.

'You'd be amazed what a tremendous upheaval it can be, turning a house as large as that into a hospital. Practically everything has to go into storage and new plumbing installed. Most of the large rooms such as the dining-room and the drawing-room became wards and the library a recreation room. Can you imagine doing that with Edenthorpe?'

'So many large houses were turned into hospitals, but the task of putting everything back as it was must be horrendous.'

'Yes. Thankfully Stanfield is almost back to normal.'

'And will you stay on?'

Having finished her meal, Cordelia placed her napkin on the table, lowering her gaze, suddenly uncomfortable at being asked the question she had agonised over for days now. 'I—I don't think so. It—it's just that it's too much like Edenthorpe—everything I've tried to get away from,' she said hesitantly, unable to give the real reason why she was considering leaving—even though it would be the most painful thing she had ever done.

Her father was not deceived and frowned suspiciously.

A hurt expression covered her mother's face. 'You have much to be grateful for, Cordelia. You were fortunate to be brought up in a house like Edenthorpe.'

Cordelia looked contrite. 'I know. I'm sorry—but you know what I mean, Mother. It isn't Edenthorpe itself, it's the old established order of things—of what is thought to be proper—that I object to. I'm thinking of returning to London and trying to get a position in some government office. I did so enjoy working in Whitehall that final year of the War. Now I'm better qualified, I might be able to get a secretarial post with a Member of Parliament, or something to that effect.'

'Well—I do have plenty of connections at Westminster,' said her father. 'If I can be of help, you know I'd be only too happy to.'

'I know—and thank you, Father. But you know I'd rather make my own way.'

There was a moment's silence while her father studied her seriously. Her face had become strangely vulnerable all of a sudden. 'What is wrong, Cordelia? I know there is something. You've not been yourself since you arrived for the wedding. Does it have anything to do with your employer by any chance?'

'Why—no,' she said, laughing nervously, becoming conscious of a sudden feeling of alarm. 'Of course not. Why on earth should you think that?'

Her father's eyes narrowed. 'I don't know. You tell me. What is he like? Has he made any advances towards you?'

Cordelia stared at him aghast. 'Of course he

hasn't. He's too much of a gentleman to compromise his secretary. It would scarcely be conducive to a proper working relationship.'

'You may be protective of your newfound independence, Cordelia, but you are still my daughter. By entering what has always been a male-dominated world, because of your sex you are likely to be taken advantage of. You are very dear to me and if anything is amiss then I wish to know about it. Tell me what he's like—your employer.'

There was a stern quality to her father's voice which filled Cordelia with unease, making her regret she'd ever mentioned anything about Stanfield Hall.

'There's little to tell, really. I think he's about thirty-two or thirty-three years of age, extremely wealthy—and he fought in the army during the War—reaching the rank of captain. He—he is extremely interested in horses—racehorses, in particular.'

'I see. He seems like a man after my own heart,' said her father with a certain irony. 'And are you in love with him?'

The question was asked in such a forthright manner that Cordelia could only sit and stare at him, aghast.

'Well?'

'Oh—I—I don't know,' she floundered, beginning to tremble, feeling her face hot and flushed beneath his icy stare. 'All I know is that I cannot go on working for him—feeling as I do,' she said quietly, lowering her eyes, unable to meet his penetrating gaze.

Her father nodded, beginning to understand the situation perfectly. 'I see. And how do you think he feels about you?'

'Really, Father, that I—I cannot say.'

'Does he have a wife or a fiancée?'

'No. He—he was married but his wife was killed in an air raid on London.'

'So—he is a widower?'

'Yes.'

'And how would you feel if you were to discover he felt the same way about you, Cordelia?' asked her mother gently.

Cordelia turned her head slowly and looked directly into her mother's face and there, plain for her to see, was a gentle understanding she had rarely seen before. Her mother did not care to show emotion of any kind if she could help it.

'From what you have told us he sounds a decent enough gentleman. Would it really be such a bad thing to settle down?'

'Yes, it would. It's not what I want. Not yet. There's too much I want to do before I settle down with anyone.' Sighing deeply, she stood up and pushed her chair back. 'Please excuse me. I promised myself an early night. I shall have to make an early start tomorrow if I'm to return to Stanfield.'

'You will keep us informed about what transpires between you and this—what is your employer's name, by the way?' her father asked, rising from his chair and going to stand beside his wife who was about to pour him a brandy.

'Frankland,' Cordelia said absently, making her way to the door. 'Alex Frankland.'

There was a sudden, deathlike silence in the room. It was so profound that it was almost audible. Cordelia did not see the look that came over her parents' faces—disbelief, incredulity and shock. It was a small agonised sound made by her mother that made her turn towards them. Her parents were staring at her, their faces ashen—as if they had received some mortal wound. She saw her mother's hand reach out and clutch that of her father. Neither of them moved.

Slowly Cordelia moved towards them, her eyes moving from one to the other, a curious tightness beginning around her heart, feeling a chill of terror shiver through her, making her suspect that something was terribly wrong.

'Why—whatever is the matter? Do you know Captain Frankland?'

Quickly her parents seemed to pull themselves together. 'No—of course not,' said her father, clearing his throat nervously. 'It was the name—that's all. It seemed familiar.'

'Familiar?' asked Cordelia, bemused.

'Yes. For—for a moment we—we thought you said Franklyn.'

'There was someone in Billy's regiment called Franklyn,' her mother explained quickly. 'He—he was killed in France, too. It just made us think of Billy—that's all. His death is still so very painful for us both to remember.'

Cordelia was not convinced that they were speaking the truth—although why they should feel the need to cover anything up was quite beyond her. 'I know, and I suppose the names do sound alike.' She gave them both a puzzled look before leaning over and kissing each of them goodnight. When she reached the door her mother's voice halted her.

'Does Captain Frankland know who you are, Cordelia?'

'No. I am just plain and simple Delia King and he need never be any the wiser.'

'No—indeed,' whispered her mother, watching her daughter leave the room before turning her stricken face to her husband. 'I told you we should have told her the truth from the start. Do you think we ought to tell her before she leaves in the morning?'

'No. It's too late. If she has no intention of telling him who she is, then there is every chance he'll not find out. At least—let us pray that he doesn't.'

* * *

From then until Cordelia left for Norfolk the following morning, there was an atmosphere of crisis at Edenthorpe which transmitted itself to her. All the peace and tranquillity that had accumulated over the years since Billy's death vanished and a new element of fear came to haunt them that would not be dispelled until Cordelia had left Stanfield Hall and the employ of Alex Frankland.

Cordelia was deeply suspicious, feeling there was a secret at Edenthorpe that no one spoke of, and it was something which brought her a great deal of unease as she set off on her long journey back to Stanfield Hall.

Chapter Eight

Cordelia was met at the station by Maxine, who was surprised to see her for she was not expected back until the following day. When they reached the house Maxine left to attend to some fête or other and Alex, unaware of Cordelia's return, was at the stables. Feeling the need for some exercise after her long drive, and eager to see him again—although she was deluding herself if she rejected this as being the true reason why she suddenly decided to take a ride—she hurried to her room to change.

When she arrived in the stable yard Alex was standing with his back to her, leaning against the lower half of a stable door, peering inside at a new addition to his stables. Cordelia paused for a moment to observe him, suddenly realising how much she had missed him. She hadn't seen him for a week but it seemed like a whole lifetime.

He was bare headed and for once his black hair was tousled; his white shirt and fawn-coloured breeches, tucked into his well-worn brown riding boots, were rumpled and soiled, which told her that for most of the day he had been happily employed with his horses.

In her delight at seeing him again she moved across the yard, drawn to him irresistibly. Alex did not see her at once, then suddenly he turned, watching her in her riding habit walking towards him over the cobbled yard which shone after the recent rain with an unearthly brilliance matching her wonderful hazel eyes.

She moved towards him, a smile on her lips. Alex's eyes opened wide with pleasure and surprise on seeing her, for he hadn't expected her back at Stanfield either. He'd missed her more than he realised.

'Ah, Miss King. It's good to see you back—and dressed for riding I see.'

'Yes. It's been a long journey. I felt the need of some exercise.'

'I'd accompany you but, as you can see,' he said, indicating his soiled clothes, 'I'm hardly dressed for it. Your sister's wedding went well, I trust?'

'Yes,' Cordelia replied, glancing over the stable door at a dark brown head and inquisitive bluey-black eyes. 'Is that your recent acquisition?'

'Yes. A yearling. Come and take a look.'

After instructing one of the stable boys to saddle the mare Cordelia usually rode, he opened the stable door and they went inside. As she brushed past him he caught a faint smell of the soft subtle perfume she wore before it was overpowered by the familiar smells of the stables, of warm straw and horses.

'I went to an auction in Newmarket to look at another horse, but when I saw this young colt he appealed to me from the start. I couldn't resist buying him.'

Cordelia could see why when she saw the colt. He was a wonderful rich dark brown, getting darker towards the extremities. A startling white blaze ran down his head and he had four white socks. The bits of straw stuck to his back indicated he had been rolling. He twitched his ears and swished his tail, trustingly moving forward to inspect the newcomer, cheekily beginning to nibble Cordelia's sleeve. Laughing softly, she gently shoved him away and rubbed his velvety nose.

'He's beautiful,' she gasped with pleasure. 'He has a wonderful set of limbs and a good head.'

'And the indefinable stamp of class and breeding,' said Alex with a note of pride. 'I'm convinced, with the right training, he has the makings of a good racehorse.'

'I hope you're right. Have you thought of a name for him?'

'Not yet,' he replied, looking at her across the horse's back, distracted by the perfect picture she made in the light shining through the wooden slats of the small window, which cast an aura over her. He met her wide hazel eyes, noticing their absurdly long dark lashes.

Desire stirred within him and he wished, not for the first time, that she were not his secretary. Had she been anyone else, he would have taken her in his arms long before now and kissed her full, soft mouth and pulled her down onto the straw, its warm, animal smell having strong, primitive connotations, and made love to her.

Meeting his eyes, Cordelia's mind was attuned to his and she was suddenly conscious that they were alone in the warm, intimate confines of the small stable, where the only sounds to be heard were the soft rustles of straw as the horses shifted in their stalls.

'How is the organisation for the hunt coming along?' she asked, suddenly thinking how well he would get on with her father. They had so many things in common—and he was certainly the kind of man her mother would approve of.

'Very well. I hope you still intend taking part?'

'Yes, although I'm not yet familiar with the countryside.'

'Don't worry. You will be perfectly safe with me. I—thought you might have had second thoughts.'

'Oh? Why should I?'

'Considering your views on chasing the fox,' he said, his words softly spoken and quite uncritical.

'I know, but there's little I can do about that.'

'I suppose we could have a drag hunt—in which case the hounds follow an artificial scent.'

'I do know what drag hunting is,' she said with a touch of indignation, 'and I approve of it. But unfortunately I am in a minority.'

'That is so, I'm afraid,' he agreed, resting his arms on the colt's back, who was content to stand quite still for the moment while Cordelia continued to caress his nose.

'I doubt anyone would turn up if they knew they were not in pursuit of a fox but simply an artificial drag line. The truth is, there is nothing to compare with riding a high-spirited, courageous horse in the hunt. Hunting is one of man's oldest activities—when they would hunt not for sport but for food. I think it brings out all the primitive instincts in the hunter. It's the thrill of it, the exhilaration of the chase ending in the final capture and subjugation of its prey.'

Cordelia stared at him, blushing crimson, having a distinct feeling he was not speaking of the fox but of herself, and she was aware and hopelessly appalled that she was unable to work up any indignation. His voice was low and he looked deeply into her eyes, knowing she had interpreted his words in the way they had been intended; he smiled without contrition.

They stood motionless for what seemed a long time but it was, in fact, little more than a few seconds of highly charged emotion. They were aware of nothing else but each other and the dangerous current of attraction flowing between them. When Cordelia had gone to Edenthorpe, she had hoped a week away from him might cure her of the love she felt, which was rapidly becoming an obsession, but it had only succeeded in intensifying it.

At that moment the stable boy's head appeared over the bottom half of the door to tell Cordelia he had finished saddling her horse. She turned from Alex's intense gaze in confusion and thanked him, grateful for the interruption. Moving with the supple grace of an animal, Alex followed her out into the yard to where her horse stood waiting.

Keeping her eyes lowered, she pulled on her gloves, aware of him standing close behind her, so close she could feel the warmth of his body. Instead of holding out his hands for her foot to hoist her up onto the horse, he placed them about her waist, steady and firm, lifting her with ease into the saddle, making her acutely aware of his strength and complete masculinity.

Cordelia looked down at him as he placed her foot in the stirrup and his grey eyes met hers. There was a faint smile on his lips as he stepped back, for he was well satisfied that he had been able to reduce her to such confusion. He was prepared to expend all his patience in breaking down her barricades, for he sensed that beneath her cool exterior she had a true capacity for love.

'Have a pleasant ride,' he said softly.

As Cordelia rode off she knew he was watching her. She chided herself severely: she must try and pull herself together. All of a sudden she felt completely out of control of her life. It was like being swept along into the heart of a hurricane. She trembled slightly. After all, she was flesh and blood and not immune to Alex's sexual magnetism, but how much longer were they going to be able to deny the strong physical attraction that was drawing them together?

James and Diana arrived at Stanfield Hall the day before the meet. Because there was to be considerable hunting in the area over the next two weeks, James had come equipped with three of his best hunters, one for Diana and two for himself. Like a lot of keen huntsmen, he considered it essential to have two horses a day. One good horse could doubtless manage a day, or most of it, but the distances covered, and the constant galloping and jumping, imposed a severe strain on a hunter.

That evening, Alex insisted on Cordelia joining them for dinner. Usually she had one of the maids take her meal up to her room, which she would have preferred to do that evening, but after much persuasion from James and Maxine she had finally relented.

She found it difficult being with Alex of late, and throughout the evening she avoided his eyes for she found it hard to look at him, and there was something in his voice when he spoke to her that made it hard for her to answer him.

Ever since the day in the stables when she had returned from Edenthorpe he had a way of making her feel distinctly uncomfortable whenever she was with him. He was the only man who had ever looked at her with such cool calculation, as if he were a lion and she a fawn he would pounce on when he was good and ready.

Aware of Diana's hostility towards her—she clearly resented sitting down to a meal with one of the staff, for in the world in which she lived class and distinction were still to be observed—Cordelia was mostly quiet throughout the meal, content to listen to the conversation with a polite interest, conscious that Diana tried to exclude her from any discussion.

Talk was of things in general and the few days James and Diana had spent at their chateau near Rouen. They also talked of horses, the main topic being the following day's hunt.

'Are you looking forward to the hunt, James?' asked Cordelia when the remains of the meal had been cleared away and they were sitting comfortably. She looked to where he was slouched against the cushions on the settee, trying desperately to keep his eyes open.

With a heavy lock of blond hair falling over his brow and his lips curved in a smile, it gave him an angelic look which made him look like a small boy. Having imbibed of too much wine before and during dinner, and too much port afterwards, he was in danger of falling asleep.

Alex smiled indulgently across at his friend. 'If you mean does he show off a bit by riding the most powerful stallion, jumping the most—and highest—fences and risking life and limb more than anyone else,' he said, 'then yes, he will be.'

'James is a superb horseman, isn't he, Alex?' murmured Diana, looking across at him from where she was sitting elegantly in an armchair.

'Absolutely. He rides with the Quorn in Leicestershire,' he explained to Cordelia, who was sitting beside Maxine on a settee close to the fire.

'Which is hunting's paradise,' said James suddenly, slurring his words and, with an effort, half-opening his sleepy blue eyes, lifting his arm up in the air in an exaggerated gesture to demonstrate the truth of this. 'The 'shire's the capital of fox-hunting in England. All else is provincial—merely second-best—or worse. You do agree, don't you, Alex?'

Alex smiled good humouredly across at him as

his head flopped against the back of the settee. 'Well, tomorrow, James, I'm afraid you'll have to be content with second-best. Here in Norfolk we cannot hope to compete with the enormous crowds of mounted followers as is the case with the Quorn—especially on the more popular days. Although I am expecting a good turn out. I don't believe you will be disappointed—unless, of course, you wake up with a frightful hangover.'

'He won't be disappointed. James has brought two of his finest hunters, Alex,' said Diana. 'If it is to be a long day then, in his view, there is no better tonic after a tiring run than to mount a fresh horse.'

'I agree absolutely, for I am certain more horses injure themselves when they are tired at the end of the day. Although I think tomorrow's hunt will be over by four o'clock at the latest.'

'Will you be joining the hunt, Miss King?' asked Diana, watching Cordelia like a hostile cat.

'Yes. However, I shall not be in on the kill. I intend turning back at some point. There are bound to be a lot of people returning to the house afterwards and I would like to give Maxine a hand with the preparations.'

'You don't have to,' said Alex. 'We do have servants to do that.'

'I know, but I'd like to. Really.'

'Don't tell me you're one of those people who

are against fox hunting, Miss King?' said Diana imperiously.

'It is not my idea of a pleasurable pastime, if that is what you mean. But, if you don't mind, I prefer not to discuss it. Captain Frankland is aware of how I feel.'

Diana's eyes narrowed. 'I'm sure he is. However, it's hardly a pastime but a way of life—as it has been for generations past.'

Determined to keep calm Cordelia looked her in the eye. 'That doesn't mean to say it is right.'

'But everyone enjoys it—you only have to ask them—riders and hounds alike.'

Cordelia had to admit that she enjoyed riding hell for leather in the open countryside as much as anyone else, but she couldn't help saying, with a delicate lift to her eyebrows, 'Then it's a pity no one thought to ask the fox.'

Two angry red spots appeared on Diana's cheeks and she pursed her lips. Knowing that she was silently fuming, trying desperately to control her temper for fear she made a fool of herself, Cordelia exchanged looks with Alex and he grinned lazily, frankly amused by the short interchange between them. However, sensing a skirmish, Maxine stood up.

Maxine did not much care for Diana. There was something malicious about her and it was obvious that she didn't like and was terribly jealous of Delia. She had been angling for Alex ever since

Pamela had died—it was plain by the way she always trailed around with her brother.

Oh, she had the right sort of background—she was rich and beautiful and extremely wealthy—but since the War all that didn't seem to matter to Alex anymore. But he was a gentleman and, as James was his closest friend, he always played the perfect host. Besides, Maxine thought, glancing with warmth down at Cordelia, she could see his attentions were taken with someone a little closer to home.

'If you young people will forgive me, I think I'll go to bed. It's likely to be a long day tomorrow and there will be much to do.'

'I think I'll come with you, Maxine,' said Cordelia, also rising. She looked at James, who had finally succumbed to tiredness and was snoring softly. 'I think James may need a hand to climb the stairs when he eventually decides to go to bed.'

'Goodnight,' said Maxine, going out and leaving the door open for Cordelia.

'Goodnight, Maxine. Won't you stay and have a nightcap?' Alex asked Cordelia as she was about to follow her.

She looked to where he was sitting, completely relaxed with a drink in his hand, his hair falling forward attractively over his brow.

'No. Thank you. I am rather tired and there are one or two things I have to do. Please excuse me.'

'By all means,' said Diana. 'We do not wish to keep you from your work, Miss King.'

Cordelia turned and looked her straight in the eye. 'You won't do that. Goodnight.'

Cordelia didn't go to bed straight away for she was tense and restless and didn't feel much like sleeping. After hearing everyone come up to bed, when the great house was quiet, she left her room and silently made her way down to the kitchens where she poured herself a glass of milk.

Not feeling like going back to her room, she wandered away from the main part of the house towards the recently refurbished music room, which had long French windows overlooking the lawns. The curtains had not been drawn and the room was lit by the silvery light of the moon.

Closing the door softly behind her, she placed her glass of milk on top of the grand piano, switching on the light next to it and raising the piano lid, idly letting her fingers trail over the ivory keys.

Unable to resist the urge to play and realising she had no audience, she sat on the piano stool and automatically began to play a Chopin's nocturne, softly so as not to disturb the slumbering household, closing her eyes and becoming immersed in the music, the notes coming to her like crystal clear drops of water. Immediately she began to relax, the music releasing her from some deep unconscious anxiety.

She played with a degree of feeling which seemed to carry her away—far beyond the walls of the room. It was a feeling almost beyond her control.

She did not hear the door open and Alex enter the room, closing it softly behind him. She was only aware of his presence when he stood behind her. Sensing she was about to stop playing, he moved to stand beside the piano—resting his arms on its top and looking at her closely.

'No—don't stop. I would like to listen.'

Cordelia continued playing, at last, no longer afraid to look at him, meeting his eyes. The expression in them was unforgettable. He was looking at her with such a passionate intensity which, combined with the music, began to awaken all her senses, making her conscious of only this moment which was suspended in time.

It was as if it had become identified with the music, for everything that had gone before and everything that was to come were irrelevant as they became as one in an enchanted circle. Alex was looking at her as no man had ever looked at her before, and she had never felt drawn to any man as she was to him.

When the last notes of the nocturne faded and died away, she let her hands fall into her lap, feeling it had sapped her will. There was complete silence inside the room. Both were reluctant to break the magic of the moment which had held them in thrall. The intensity of Alex's gaze held Cordelia spellbound, weaving an invisible cord about her from which there was no escape—from which she had no desire to escape, until at last he smiled softly.

'That was beautiful, Miss King. You play well. Another of your many accomplishments. You really are a talented young woman.'

'Thank you.'

'I was sorry you decided to leave us so abruptly earlier.'

'I'm sorry. I did not mean to seem abrupt. I—I had one or two things to do for tomorrow.'

Alex sighed. 'You know, Miss King, you take your work too seriously. You really should learn to relax.'

Perhaps he was right, she thought. She was too serious. When she had first come to Stanfield Hall she had been confident in her own future, hoping it would be a stepping stone to her career—a place where she could gain experience in her work. What she had not expected was that she would come to love the place—or that her work would become complicated by her feelings for Alex.

'You may be right,' she smiled. 'But my work is important to me.'

'And it is a credit to you. I hope Diana did not

upset you with her remarks about hunting earlier?'

Cordelia smiled. 'It would take more than Diana's remarks to upset me.'

'I'm glad to hear it.'

'However—I have a distinct feeling that she does not like me.'

'Perhaps she has good reason.'

'Does she?'

'I believe it to be a simple matter of jealousy, Miss King.'

Cordelia flushed. 'Then she has no reason to be.'

'Hasn't she? Oh, I think she has.' He sighed deeply. 'Diana is James's sister, which at times makes it extremely difficult for me. I am not unaware that she would like me to pay her more attention than I do.'

'And you don't want to?'

'No.' He moved away from her, going to stand by the French windows and looking out over the sloping lawns, bathed in the moon's silvery sheen. 'Why have you been eluding me of late, Miss King?'

Taken aback by the suddenness of his question, Cordelia rose and moved a little towards him, his tall, clear-cut profile etched against the light. It was true, she had been trying to avoid seeing him, but she could not say so.

'I—I was not aware that I had. Why on earth should I?'

'Perhaps you are afraid.'

'Afraid? Afraid of what?' she asked in a voice that strove to sound natural, but succeeded in only exposing her nervousness and uncertainty.

'Afraid to face up to your feelings.'

He turned to face her, seeing her cheeks flushed rose above the soft pastel pink of her dress. His gaze was compelling and there was a moment's silence in which Cordelia's heart began beating in a quite unpredictable manner.

'When you played that nocturne were you aware of how much you told me in that music? You expressed to me how you felt—and I understood because I, too, feel the same. They are feelings we have both tried to suppress for a long time. But how much longer can we continue to do so?'

His voice reached out to her and held her, but Cordelia turned from him, unable to continue looking into those hypnotic grey eyes. Alex looked at her, at her shining cap of soft golden hair, at her slender body, as delicate and supple as the stem of a flower. Irresistibly he was drawn towards her and he crossed to where she stood, standing behind her, but he did not touch her—although his fingers ached to do so.

'How much longer do we have to fence with

words? And how much longer are you going to pretend you feel nothing?'

The air between them was charged with tension. Cordelia shivered suddenly. He noticed.

'Are you cold?'

She shook her head. How could she tell him it was because he encroached too closely, that he aroused such a tempest inside her that she was afraid—afraid of herself and that she might lose control over herself—her body and emotions, completely?

'Then can you tell me that I am wrong?'

His voice died away into the silence of the room about them as he waited for her answer. Still he did not touch her but he was just behind her, so close she could feel his warm breath on her neck.

Cordelia shook her head slowly. 'No,' she whispered, her voice trembling slightly. 'No—you are not wrong.'

'I know you are dedicated to your career—but does that mean you have to exclude love?'

'Yes. When it happens to concern my employer. It—it would be highly improper.'

Very gently Alex placed his hands on her shoulders and turned her round to face him.

'Would it? Don't you think it's about time we stopped being proper? I've wanted you from the first moment I saw you—and you know it.'

He was standing very close. Cordelia could smell his skin and the faint aroma of his cologne.

His presence held her like a magnet. She swallowed hard, shaking her head in a vain attempt to resist. 'No—'

'Yes,' he insisted, his voice seductive and ever so persuasive as he lowered his head, his eyes gleaming with a sensual luminosity as they focused on her quivering, parted lips, 'just like I have known all along that you feel exactly the same.'

His lips merely brushed hers lightly, but the touch sent a wave of happiness through her. They continued to make a line of trailing kisses from her mouth down to the soft flesh of her throat and she arched her long white neck to receive them, closing her eyes, her thick dark lashes resting on her cheeks, fluttering like butterflies' wings.

'We—we can't,' protested Cordelia weakly, breathlessly, without the will to resist—and nor did she want to. 'We have an arrangement—I am your secretary. It wouldn't be right.'

'There is no reason why we have to deny how we feel,' he murmured, continuing to kiss every inch of her beautiful, fine-boned face. 'I've been very patient—wanting to give you time. But I think that time has just run out,' and so saying he wrapped his arms around her and covered her mouth with his own, feeling her lips part beneath his to receive his kiss, willingly, passionately.

Between his kisses Alex paused to murmur passionate endearments and Cordelia closed her eyes and melted against him, allowing herself to be carried away on this overwhelming wave of passion, experiencing a joy which temporarily effaced everything. They became lost in the torrent of their love and Cordelia groaned, raising her hands, slipping her fingers into his thick black hair, gripping it fiercely to bring his mouth more closely to her own.

Their kisses were deep and urgent, as if each one might be their last. Alex caressed her, sliding his long, determined fingers, as light as thistledown, down her spine and over the gentle curve of her buttocks. They seemed to burn her flesh beneath the thin material of her dress, the sensation causing a spark to flicker and flare within her, racing through her veins like liquid fire, filling her with a craving for love like she had never experienced before.

After a while Alex lifted his head, striving to control his hungry passion. He looked down into Cordelia's dark, velvety eyes, large with love and desire, glad to see he wasn't going to have to fight, for she had offered no resistance, just a calm contentment of acceptance.

'So—I was right in my suspicions, Miss King.'

'Why—what do you mean?'

'Beneath the cool exterior you present to the world, you are like a smouldering volcano,' he smiled, his eyes warmly devouring her upturned face. 'I cannot wait to witness its eruption.'

'I'm afraid you'll have to,' she whispered, pulling back slightly within the intimate circle of his arms, seeing the tenderness filling his eyes. 'This—this is all so unexpected.'

'Is it?'

She sighed. 'No. Not really. But I do need time to think—to put everything into perspective. I—I never meant this to happen. I have tried so hard to avoid it.'

'I don't think it's what either of us planned but it was inevitable—feeling as we do.' He pulled her back into his arms, drawing her close until her body moulded against his, finding her lips once more and kissing her long and deep. She clung to him like ivy clings to a tree, his long lean body giving her a promise of pleasure such as she had never imagined.

'I love you, Miss King,' he whispered, his mouth against hers. 'I want you with me always. Fate decreed our paths should cross that night in London when our cars almost collided, and throughout all the weeks you have been at Stanfield I have watched you, wanting you. Being near you day after day and not being able to touch you for fear you might take flight has nearly driven me insane. What is there to think about?'

'Cordelia gazed wonderingly into his eyes, seeing there the truth of his words. 'And I love you, very much,' she whispered, her words uncomplicated by thought. 'It is something I have been aware of for a very long time. But this changes everything between us—don't you see?' she whispered, suddenly afraid that, because of what she had to say, she was in danger of losing his love, which had been hers for so brief a moment.

Alex's eyes hardened suddenly but he did not release his hold of her. 'No, I don't see. What are you trying to say?'

'That I can no longer go on working for you here at Stanfield. It—it just wouldn't be right—feeling as we do for each other. You must understand that I have worked hard to achieve my independence. I—I cannot just abandon it now.'

'I understand how you must feel but I am not asking you to abandon anything—although why you feel you have to leave Stanfield I really cannot understand. You are happy here? You like the work, don't you?'

'Yes. You know I do.'

'Then why talk of leaving, for heaven's sake?' Again he held her close. 'Oh, Delia,' he murmured against her hair, speaking her name for the first time. 'You possess such innocence. Sometimes you are as transparent as day and yet, at others, as dark and mysterious as night—with a confidence and wisdom way beyond your years. What are we going to do? I cannot let you go.'

Held within his arms, Cordelia's heart almost ceased to beat. She stared at him, filled with indecision. Alex took her chin between his fingers and raised her head so the light shone in her wonderful darkly glowing eyes.

'Well, Miss King? What have you to say?'

Cordelia slid her arms about his neck and drew his face once more down to hers, her lips warm and moist as they tenderly caressed his own. 'This is too important a matter to deal with at this time of night,' she murmured. 'I think we should wait and see what tomorrow brings.'

Together they went towards the hall and up the stairs, neither of them aware, as they kissed each other goodnight, of the watching eyes from the slightly open door at the end of the landing. Only when Cordelia had gone inside her room and Alex had disappeared into his own did Diana close the door and lean against it, breathing hard, shocked by what she had just witnessed, both furious and frightened that she might lose Alex, the man she wanted for herself, to his secretary.

Chapter Nine

Back in her room Cordelia tried to put her confused thoughts into some kind of order. She sighed deeply, lying in the warm cocoon of her sheets, feeling again the pressure of Alex's lips on hers, unable to believe all that had happened, all he had said. Had she foreseen what would happen when she went to get a glass of milk, would she have gone? she asked herself, suddenly finding that she was faced with a dilemma, for what had happened had changed everything.

Now she would have to make Alex aware of her true identity. Maybe he wouldn't be angry with her for deceiving him when he realised why she'd had to resort to subterfuge.

But then a thought occurred to her. He hadn't mentioned marriage, so she might not have to tell him. Perhaps he considered her to be beneath him socially and his intentions did not stretch beyond an affair. And wouldn't that be better for her? At least it would enable her to continue with her career, even though she would have to seek another position, for one thing was clear—she could not go on working for him at Stanfield any longer.

Being apart from Alex for any length of time would be a terrible wrench, but better that than she never see him again. This was unthinkable and she thrust the unpleasant thought out of her mind.

But was she right in contemplating embarking on a love affair? If her parents were to find out, they would be horrified. This was her first and, she was convinced—in the afterglow of his embrace—her last real love. In the past she had only ever experienced schoolgirl infatuations. She had never been in love or had a serious relationship with any man.

The following morning Cordelia was up early. The house was in chaos as servants rushed about all over the place, making preparations for the hunt and refreshments for the guests afterwards. She was told Alex had already gone to the stables, which was a relief, for she preferred not to face him while her mind was still in such confusion.

On her way to the office she stopped to pick a bundle of newspapers up from the hall table, which someone had delivered from the local newsagents the previous afternoon. Idly she thumbed through them, that month's copy of the *Tatler* catching her eye. Feeling a curious sense of foreboding she opened it, slowly turning the pages filled with pictures of the past month's news on society events.

Her mouth went dry and she went cold all over when at last she saw her face staring out at her from between the pages, along with those of her parents and Emily and her husband at their wedding. She groaned inwardly for she should have known that a publication reporting such a prestigious wedding, which would have appeared in several newspapers and magazines, would be sure to turn up at Stanfield.

Not that Alex read society magazines, but Maxine liked to look through them. Her parents had been featured regularly in the past, as had her sisters and David, but not since she had been a child had she been featured, so until now she had not been afraid of being recognised.

So engrossed was she in the magazine that she failed to see that Diana had paused on her way down the stairs and was watching her closely.

Quickly Cordelia rolled the magazine up and went into the office, unaware that Diana passed the open doorway just in time to see her dispose of the offending magazine in the wastepaper basket.

It was later, when Cordelia had left the office, that Diana went inside to retrieve it, quickly flicking through the pages until she came to the one which had so clearly upset Cordelia. After reading the announcement and digesting the picture, Diana's face expressed a look of malicious triumph.

'Well—well,' she said to herself, tucking the magazine under her arm. 'Who would have thought it?'

After changing into her riding habit, Cordelia went to the stables for the horse. One of the stable lads was just leading her out and helped her to mount. The yard was a hive of activity, the air charged with tremendous excitement as horses were led out and saddled up. Hunt followers were beginning to arrive in force and vehicles and trailers littered the yards and roads all around Stanfield.

Cordelia's breath caught in her throat when she saw Alex across the yard from her. He was bareheaded and superbly handsome and was just finishing tightening the girths on his huge black stallion. His cream breeches fitted him to perfection and there was not a crease in his pink coat which emphasised his lean, muscular body. His stock was smooth and snowy white, highlighting his bronzed good looks.

He swung himself up into the saddle with perfect ease, his riding boots gleaming like glass. One of the stable boys passed him his black riding hat, which he placed on his smooth dark hair.

'Should last the day, sir,' he said to his master. 'He's had plenty of exercise—seen to it myself.'

'Good lad,' said Alex, turning at that moment and catching Cordelia's appraising eye.

Cordelia saw his face quicken and felt her heart give a sudden leap. He trotted over to her, stopping beside her, his eyes on her face, his expression serious and at the same time inquiring.

'Good morning. You slept well?' he said in a quiet voice.

'Eventually. I think the milk helped.'

'You look wonderful this morning. I've been thinking of you,' he said for her ears alone, his eyes, watching the movement of her lips, far more eloquent than his speech.

'Thank you,' she replied, feeling the blood rush to her face, remembering the previous night and finding it difficult to appear calm and unconcerned at the memory of his embrace—and how she suddenly found herself wishing they were alone now so he could repeat the action. 'You rose early.'

'I'm an old campaigner. Once the sun has risen I find it difficult to sleep. Are you looking forward to the hunt?'

'Yes. Fortunately, the weather is perfect.'

Alex turned, seeing James riding towards them.

He looked again at Cordelia. 'I hope you enjoy it. Take care, won't you? We'll talk later.'

'Here you are, Delia,' said James pulling up alongside them. 'I've been looking for you all over the place.'

They both looked at James, who looked surprisingly alert and in the best of spirits considering his overindulgence of the previous evening.

'I say, you look extremely fetching, Delia. Do hope you're going to stay near me in the hunt.'

'No,' she laughed. 'I prefer to be near the back, if you don't mind, James.'

'Oh, well, suit yourself,' he said. 'Come along. Let's go and join the others. They're coming round with the stirrup cup. Wouldn't want to miss that,' he laughed with a humorous wink at Alex. 'Diana will be among them somewhere.'

With a quick look at Alex, Cordelia left the yard with James, trotting towards the front of the house where riders were beginning to congregate, the mixture of black coats and hunting pink making a splendid sight. They rode among them, reaching out and taking a glass of punch from the tray of one of the servants.

Near the fence of an adjoining field, they saw the pack of hounds being kept in control by the whippers-in and hunt servants. They were restless, baying and yelping in excitement, impatient for the action to begin.

'So here you both are,' said a clear voice.

Turning, Cordelia found herself looking into Diana's dark eyes. She was an attractive sight in her habit, sitting her horse with a straight-backed, easy grace, riding side-saddle like all the other ladies taking part in the hunt.

'Do you enjoy hunting, Miss King?'

Cordelia stared at her in surprise for it was a rarity for Diana to seek a conversation with her. 'Yes—although I haven't hunted for quite some time.'

'Of course not. None of us have—what with the War and everything. I believe you have some good fox hunting areas in Yorkshire, with good open conditions where a hunt can be easily seen. I rode with the Zetland once which I enjoyed enormously. Who do you ride with, Miss King?'

She was watching Cordelia closely, her eyes narrowed with malicious enjoyment, suddenly making Cordelia feel decidedly uneasy, for she felt there were hidden connotations behind her question.

'Oh—the Bramham Moor—and I have ridden with the Middleton on occasion. Both areas have great variety.'

'My! You *have* been around, haven't you? I'm rather envious. Does your father keep horses?'

'Yes—a few.'

'Racehorses?'

Cordelia glanced at her sharply. 'Why do you ask?'

Diana shrugged, giving the impression that it was of little interest to her and that she was merely trying to make polite conversation. But Cordelia sensed otherwise and was becoming suspicious.

'Oh—no reason. Only it costs money to keep and train horses—we know that, don't we, James? To do so one must be reasonably wealthy,' she said, casually taking a proffered glass of punch and beginning to sip it with great relish, savouring every mouthful—as she was Cordelia's answers to her questions—to which she already knew the answers.

Cordelia stared at her, colour flooding her cheeks at the unexpectedness of this conversation. There was something different in Diana's manner towards her which was beginning to make her feel uneasy, and she wondered at its cause. James came to her rescue.

'I say, Diana—that's rather rude. The financial affairs of Delia's father hardly concern you.'

'Please, James—let your sister finish,' said Cordelia, remaining calm, eyeing Diana steadily.

'Oh—I know it's none of my business,' Diana continued in honeyed tones. 'It's just that I find it rather curious—and strange—that someone from a well-off background should find the need to do such menial work.'

Cordelia laughed, and her laughter was so light and genuine that Diana boiled with sudden savagery but, knowing she had it within her power to make Cordelia Hamilton-King laugh on the other side of her face when she thought it in her own best interests to do so, she felt a sudden surge of triumph and managed to bring a smile to her lips.

'On the contrary—I do not consider what I do menial—in fact I enjoy it,' said Cordelia, giving no sign that she was disconcerted or intimidated by Diana. She would not give her the satisfaction. But she was wondering what could have prompted this sudden interest in her affairs.

Feeling her horse becoming restless, she dragged her eyes from Diana's coolly speculative gaze and looked around her, seeing the hunt was about to move off. 'I think the hunt's about to start.' Thankful for the excuse to put an end to the conversation, she began to follow the other riders.

Passing the crowds of people who had gathered to watch the start of the hunt, following the Hunt Master, they galloped off over the well-grassed country, heading towards a distant wood to draw the first covert of the day.

The air was fresh and exhilarating and Cordelia breathed it in deep, delighting in the feel of the horse moving beneath her. Nothing could compete with the thrill of riding to hounds. The sun shone and trees, shedding their leaves and carpeting the ground with an autumnal glory, cast long blue shadows over the land drenched and sparkling with early morning dew.

It was ten minutes before the pack picked up their first scent. When they heard the hounds screaming promisingly through the covert and the huntsman blowing the horn, the excited 'Heroosh' of the chase exerted a powerful spell over all the followers. Liver, black and white, followed by a sea of horses topped with scarlet and black, poured over the land, clearing hedges and leaping ditches with a fluidity reminiscent of a river in full flow.

Hunting demanded good horsemanship and skill to outwit the fox and some of the hedges and ditches were a severe test for horse and rider. Deep, broad ditches, lying in thick thorn hedges, made a formidable jump which could be tackled safely by really bold horses, but the horse that hesitated lost impetus and all too easily crashed into the ditch.

The hunt was in full cry, with riders' faces as red as their coats. Looking ahead towards the pack, Cordelia could see and hear that nothing could disguise their ferocity as they clamoured for blood.

She spotted Alex out in front, riding well in a class of his own, at one with his horse, leaping with absolute confidence over hedges and ditches. The pace of the hunt was fast and Cordelia could feel her mare beginning to tire. Never intending to stay with the hunt, she was considering pulling out when she sensed someone riding right on the heels of her horse. She wanted to pull up, but dare not for fear of colliding.

As the rider behind persisted in following close, Cordelia became angry, for over-riding was one of the worst sins in the hunting field—and one of the easiest methods of maiming or even killing the rider in front.

She could see a big, open ditch which yawned ahead of her like a chasm. She would like to have followed the lead of other riders, but because of the persistence of the rider behind she had to swerve off course, approaching the ditch at its widest point. Her experience told her that falls which occurred in ditches were seldom serious—unless taken at speed, and that was exactly what she was about to do.

Unable to check her stride, she had no choice but to gallop straight at it, making an unsound take off. As the horse landed on the other side of the ditch it stumbled badly on the soft edge. Frantically it fought to regain its footing, but Cordelia, one of her feet having lost its stirrup, was unseated and thrown. Helplessly she was somersaulted through the air and into the ditch, falling heavily and hitting her head on some loose rocks.

The last thing she saw before darkness engulfed her was Diana sitting on her horse, looking down at her from what seemed to be a great height, her lips curved in a satisfied smile.

* * *

Cordelia floated in and out of consciousness as she was transported back to Stanfield Hall and up to her room, where a deeply concerned Maxine immediately sent for the doctor. She was suffering from mild concussion and had sustained a nasty gash to her head which, although bleeding profusely, did not require suturing. The doctor advised her to remain in bed for twenty-four hours but Cordelia, now fully conscious and feeling a good deal better, apart from a frightful headache, was anxious to be up.

Her fall did not interfere with the hunt and Alex was not made aware of it until it was over and he had arrived back at Stanfield to play host to his guests—all eager to partake of the generous assortment of refreshments. The crisp air of the countryside always gave them an appetite after the hunt. Even though nothing had been killed that day—except time—they were all in exuberant spirits.

Alex had missed Cordelia's presence but she had told him that she didn't intend staying with the hunt so he assumed she had returned to the house. It was Maxine who told him of her fall, when she managed to get him away from his guests.

At once his eyes were alert with concern. 'What did you say?'

'That Delia was thrown from her horse during

the hunt. Unfortunately she landed in a ditch, hitting her head rather badly.'

'Good Lord! Why did no one tell me?'

'You were way ahead with the hunt when it happened, Alex,' said Diana, sidling into the room. 'It was fortunate I was quite near and was able to assist in getting her back to the house.'

'I must see her,' he said in alarm. 'How bad is she? Has the doctor been to see her?'

'Yes. Calm down, Alex,' ordered Maxine. 'She'll be all right when she's rested. She has a nasty cut to her face and will no doubt have a frightful headache, but apart from that she is fine. Although I have thought it might be a good idea for her to go home for a few days.'

'Yes—maybe you're right. If she agrees, I'll drive her there myself in the morning. Although I have to admit I have no idea where her parents live. The only address we have is the one in London for the flat she still shares with her friend.'

'I think I can be of help,' said Diana, producing the magazine Cordelia had been so careful to hide. Diana knew the time was right to inject her poison, knowing full well the effect it would have on Alex when he saw the awful truth about his precious secretary's background staring him in the face. 'Here—take a look.'

Alex gave her a puzzled look, for her eyes and her voice were full of something he did not care for. At first his brain was numb, for all his senses told him that something was badly wrong, that what he was about to see was not pleasant. He took the magazine from her. 'What is this?'

'Look at it and see, Alex. After you've read it and seen for yourself who she really is—then I doubt you will want to take her to her home and meet her parents.'

Slowly Alex lowered his gaze and stared at the picture of Cordelia. 'It must have been taken at her sister's wedding. I don't understand.'

'You will when you've read the name beneath the picture.'

Alex read, digesting it slowly, unable to believe what he was seeing. There was an appalled silence as he stared wordlessly at the picture which finally condemned Cordelia in his eyes. Diana watched and rejoiced with gloating eyes. In alarm Maxine went to him, for in that instant she could see he had been felled by a crippling blow.

'It would appear,' said Diana, her voice low and intense, 'that Miss King has deceived you, Alex—in the most cruel manner. What could have been her purpose, I wonder?'

Quickly Maxine took the magazine from Alex to see what it contained that had so clearly upset him. 'Dear me,' she whispered in dismay, when she too saw the picture. 'I had no idea.'

'No one had,' said Diana, excitement over the disastrous effect her revelation had caused bringing a bright glitter to her dark eyes and showing in every line of her body.

Maxine turned to her sharply. 'Please leave us, Diana,' she said curtly. 'I think you've said enough.'

'Very well,' she said and turned and left them.

Maxine looked at her nephew with concern, deeply aware of his suffering. Her heart swelled with pain. There was no softness in his expression, no emotion either, and the ice-cold slivers of steel in his eyes and the marble severity of his face left her in no doubt as to the depth of his anger.

'I am so dreadfully sorry about all this, Alex. I realise how painful it must be to have all those old wounds reopened. You must let Delia explain.'

'Don't try and defend her, Maxine,' he breathed fiercely. 'You were taken in by her just as well as I—which goes to prove that she's a better actress than either of us realised. She has an artful tongue and her powers of persuasion are quite remarkable.'

'I do not believe she came here for any vindictive reason. You must give her the chance to explain.'

'As far as I am concerned there is nothing to explain. She has betrayed me in the vilest way possible—my trust—even my love.' When he heard Maxine's gasp of surprise he fixed her with a hard stare, breathing hard. 'Yes, even that. I loved her, Maxine. I was prepared to make her my wife, no matter who she was or where she came from. But that is over—for our love could not endure such unforgivable deception.' He strode towards the door.

'Where are you going?' asked Maxine.

'To see to my guests. I've absented myself too long as it is.'

The hour was late when Cordelia awoke, the revellers having long since gone. It took her a moment to convince herself she was not still trapped in some bad dream, but as the mists of sleep began to recede she began to remember the events of the day, of her fall into the ditch and how she was certain it had been Diana who had over-ridden her, intending to cause just such an incident. If this was indeed so, then her resentment and jealousy went much deeper than she had realised.

Lifting her hand she gingerly touched the dressing the doctor has applied to the side of her face to cover the wound. She winced at the sudden pain which shot through it, remembering he had told her it was not as bad as it looked and would soon disappear. Her head ached, but she no longer felt sleepy and wondered if everyone had gone to bed.

Deciding to go and see, she slipped on a dress and hastily ran a brush through her hair before making her way down the stairs, her legs, not surprisingly, feeling a bit wobbly.

Finding the great house quiet, she was about to return to her room when she saw a faint light shining from beneath the closed door of Alex's study. Her heart stirred with delight that he might not have gone to bed with the others and, without any hesitation, she walked towards it, tapping softly and going inside, totally unprepared for what faced her.

The light in the room was dim and Alex was seated at his desk, though not working. A decanter of whisky was beside him and a half-empty glass in his hand. He was still dressed in the clothes he had worn for the hunt, with the exception of his pink coat, which had been flung carelessly over the back of a chair. His clothes were dishevelled and smudged with dirt, his stock unfastened and hanging loose at his throat.

Cordelia was about to go to him, but when he raised his head and looked at her, something in his gaze made her pause irresolutely, causing the smile to disappear from her lips. His hair hung untidily over his brow and he looked at her unsteadily, with eyes heavy with fatigue and the effects of the whisky.

When Alex saw Cordelia in the doorway, looking the perfect vision of loveliness, despite the dressing covering the wound on the side of her face, his stomach quivered and his breathing became hard in his chest. Since the moment Maxine had told him she had been hurt falling from her horse—and after being made aware of who she was—he had been fraught with a mixture of different emotions and had suffered an agony of torment, having to fight against the desire to go to her. It was only his anger and Maxine that had prevented him from doing so.

When the anger over her deceit began to burn inside him, it grew and grew with such a virulent force that he could hardly contain it. The very thought of who she was almost drove him mad. He put the glass down and rose, towering behind the desk, the light from the single lamp throwing monstrous shadows on the walls of the room. He smiled, a crooked, mocking smile, although his expression remained hard and unyielding.

'Come in,' he commanded, his tone cold, terse and impersonal, with no smile or word of affection, 'and close the door.'

With a fluttering heart Cordelia hesitated, bemused by this change in him, for the man she faced, whose voice and eyes were filled with so much anger, was not the man she knew. This was a stranger, a terrifying stranger, who filled her with fear and alarm.

He placed both his fists on the desk and leaned forward slightly. 'I said, come in.'

She did as he ordered, closing the door and moving towards the desk.

'I was sorry to hear you took a tumble this morning. However—I am glad to see you feel well enough to leave your bed,' he said coldly.

'Yes—thank you. Is—is there something wrong?'

'Since you ask—yes. Something is very wrong, Miss King—or should I say Miss Hamilton-King? Cordelia Hamilton-King, that is.' His voice was quiet, each word enunciated carefully, and the eyes that met hers were as cold as steel.

Surprise left Cordelia speechless, for it was the last thing she had expected him to say. Still—perhaps it was better that her true identity was out in the open—but it did not justify anger such as this.

'So—what am I to call you?'

'Whatever it pleases you to call me by,' she replied stiffly, suddenly finding that she was obliged to reach out and steady herself on the back of a chair as a wave of nausea swept over her. Fortunately it soon subsided, but she was aware that every muscle in her body was beginning to ache—the after-effects of the tumble she had taken, no doubt, which was hardly surprising.

So great was Alex's rage that he appeared not to notice her sudden pallor as he went on, his tone cutting. 'So—it is true?'

'Yes,' she replied, unable to see the sense in denying it. 'I need not pretend any longer.'

'Pretend? Pretend is a child's game. Deceit is a

woman's,' he sneered. 'Why did you not tell me who you were? Why did you allow me to believe you were just ordinary Delia King, when all the time you were the daughter of Lord Langhorne—one of the wealthiest men in the north of England? I am awaiting your explanation—if you have one to offer.'

'It was for precisely that reason,' Cordelia explained. 'I wanted to make my own way on my own merit—not because of who I happen to be. I wanted to be successful in my career and considered it essential that I took on my own identity. The name "Hamilton-King" is too well known in the business world.'

'How very commendable,' Alex drawled, his lips twisting with sarcasm.

Cordelia met his gaze directly. 'How did you find out who I was?'

'Diana brought the matter to my attention. She recognised you in one of the magazines—it was a picture of your sister's wedding—the major society event in the north of England for some considerable time, I believe,' he said with heavy irony.

Cordelia stared at him, understanding at last the reason for Diana's peculiar behaviour that day. She must have found the magazine she had discarded in the wastepaper basket that morning—and that picture was all it had taken to shatter the love that was growing between her and

Alex—as easily as a stone that is thrown into a pond disturbs its calm.

Anger began to flow through her, anger at herself for succumbing so readily to the embraces of this hard, cold man. She glared at him through narrowed eyes and her spine stiffened.

'So—I might have known. Did she also tell you how I happened to fall into the ditch during the hunt?'

He frowned. 'What are you saying?'

'Ask Diana. She seems to have all the answers.'

'Are you accusing her of causing your accident?'

Cordelia took a deep breath. 'Very well. I am saying that I strongly suspect she was responsible.'

'Then what you are saying is extremely serious.'

The tension between them was increasing. Cordelia stared at him, for beneath his words she could feel a violent rage fighting its way to the surface. She was beginning to suspect his anger could not be just because she had not told him her true identity. There had to be something else.

'Which, in my generosity—and because James is your closest friend—I am prepared to overlook,' she said. 'Now—will you please tell me what I have done that is so very wrong? Concealing my identity is no great crime to cause so much anger.'

Slowly, without taking his merciless eyes off hers, Alex drew himself up to his full height so that he towered above her, his body taut, and his next words were to shatter her completely.

'It concerns your brother—William Hamilton-King.'

Cordelia stared at him with huge, bewildered eyes. Suddenly she felt chilled to the marrow. 'Billy? But I don't understand. What are you saying? What has my brother to do with any of this? He—he was killed on the Western Front during the War.'

Alex's face was set hard. 'Your brother was killed in the same air raid over London that killed my wife. Her naked body was pulled from the rubble of a hotel along with that of a young officer—identified as your brother. Now do you understand what I am saying? Now do you understand why I feel nothing but hatred and contempt for the name Hamilton-King?'

Chapter Ten

As Alex threw the truth at Cordelia in so cruel a manner, he had no idea what it would do to her, that he had stripped her of something infinitely precious. All the memories she treasured of her beloved brother, the warmth and comfort that thoughts of him always gave her, had bloomed and like a flower had died. Cordelia felt her heart contract with pain and unbidden tears filled her eyes.

'No,' she whispered, shivering with the aftermath of shock and shaking her head in abject despair, once more reaching out her hand and steadying herself on the chair to keep herself from falling. 'Oh, no. What you say cannot be true. You are mistaken. You have to be mistaken.'

'It is the truth,' he said flatly, any trace of compassion he might have felt wiped from his face. Anger shimmered in every line of his tall frame.

'I will not believe it,' she cried in desperation, scalding tears beginning to run unchecked down her ashen cheeks, the pain so great she could hardly speak. Her tears now were of fear for all she stood to lose—the cherished, untarnished memories of her adored brother.

'And—and even if it was Billy's body that was pulled from the ruined hotel with that of your wife—then—then it does not mean they were having an affair. He was to have been married. He would never have done anything so dishonourable.'

'A touching tale,' scorned Alex dryly. 'Do you mean to say you knew nothing of this? I find it hard to believe.'

'Believe what you like, but I have never lied to you. I do not believe it of Billy. I will not believe it.'

'How staunchly you defend him,' he said bitterly.

'Because I knew him. I have every faith that he was innocent. He was a good man and incapable of such a thing.'

'I admire your loyalty, but I think it is somewhat misplaced.'

Cordelia stood across from him, straight and erect—as if carved from stone. She was quivering, visibly struggling against what he had told her. Suddenly she looked so frail, so fragile. The light fell softly on her face which was like a tragic mask.

The pitiful sight found a chink in Alex's armour and for a moment he weakened and almost went to her, but her next words stopped him.

'You seem to forget that I am his sister,' she said, a sudden vision of her brother, of his proud and handsome face, vivid in her mind's eye. 'I adored him like no other. Have you any idea what it was like to be told he was killed and the dreadful images that tormented me as to the manner in which he could have met his death—hearing the horrendous stories of the total carnage on the battlefields of France and Belgium?

'I have truly believed for the last four years that Billy died the honourable death of a soldier in battle and—and now you tell me this. How could you be so cruel—so totally heartless? I will have to live with this knowledge for the rest of my life.'

'I would have thought you would prefer to know the truth rather than a lie. I think you should ask your parents why they did not tell you the truth about your brother's death at the time, don't you?' Alex rasped with brutal sarcasm. 'And you seem all too ready to forget that I lost a wife.'

They stayed silent for a moment, not speaking, the awful truth and what it meant to them both stretching between them. The ordeal was proving too much for Cordelia. Once again her head began to swim with nausea and she felt the floor heave under her feet. She turned from his hard, angry gaze and stumbled towards the door where she paused, struggling to stay upright. Taking a deep breath she turned and looked at him one last time—her heart breaking.

'It is clear to me that, because of who I am, my presence offends you. Under the circumstances it would be impossible for me to continue working for you. I will leave Stanfield Hall first thing in the morning. Goodnight, Alex.'

She got no further for at that moment the room began to spin about her. Her heart began beating incredibly fast and a cold sweat broke out all over her body. Before she knew what was happening, she crumpled to the floor, descending into a swirling darkness for the second time that day.

For an instant Alex stood motionless and then, gathering his senses, he moved quickly around the desk and looked down at the girl at his feet. Pity swelled his heart, causing the demon rage that possessed him to relax its grip. Quickly he picked her up in his arms and carried her to her room, placing her gently on the bed.

His heart ached when he look down at her. She had told him she loved him and he did not doubt her love. From the moment they had met spontaneous attraction had drawn them together and now fate had stepped in and separated them in the most cruel manner. But there could be no kind of relationship, no future, for them together with this thing lying between them like some eternal obstacle.

And yet, as he fled from her bedside, leaving Maxine to watch over her, how could he forget the love and passion she aroused in him? She had bewitched him and he would have to live with that for all time.

Cordelia had felt herself being raised and carried in his strong arms up the stairs, seeing his face devoid of anything save an awful fear before she slipped back into the blackness of the abyss. Now, as she surfaced yet again when he laid her on the bed and went out of the room, she struggled to call him back, but she couldn't. With a quivering sigh she gave herself up to the darkness. Alex had gone. He no longer wanted her. She had nothing left to hope for.

She awoke with a heavy feeling of sadness, knowing she must leave Stanfield as soon as she had collected her things together. Maxine told her that Alex had ridden off on his horse at dawn in a dark and angry mood. Cordelia sighed, feeling that this was probably a blessing. It was best that she left without either of them inflicting further pain on the other. Besides, she had to see her parents, although she did not look forward to the long drive to Leeds.

Maxine tried insisting that she remained in bed—that it was sheer madness to even contemplate driving all the way to Leeds in her condition, but Cordelia refused to listen, even though she had to force herself out of bed. Her head still ached abominably, but she hadn't the time to wait for it to subside. She wanted to be gone before Alex returned to the house.

It was difficult saying goodbye to Maxine, who was deeply upset and full of regrets over the way everything had turned out. Since Cordelia had come to Stanfield the two had become extremely fond of each other. As she was about to climb into her car she heard someone crossing the drive towards her. She turned quickly, her eyes lighting up with the hope that it might be Alex, but it was James, his expression unusually grave.

'James!'

'You look as if you're leaving,' he said, having seen the hope fill her eyes, only to be replaced by disappointment when she saw it saw not Alex. Maxine had told him of what Cordelia intended, and had appealed to him to try and persuade her to remain at Stanfield until she was well enough to leave. He was as saddened as Maxine was by the whole unfortunate affair.

'Yes. Yes, I am.'

'Without saying goodbye?'

'I—I'm sorry, James. I just didn't feel like facing anyone this morning.'

'Look, Delia, I heard what happened yesterday. Diana told me.'

'Yes—she would,' said Cordelia with bitter irony.

'For what it's worth, I'm sorry,' he said gently. 'Have you seen Alex this morning?'

'No. He went riding early and isn't back yet. I doubt he would want to see me anyway.' She looked at James directly. 'You knew his wife, didn't you, James—and my brother?'

'Yes. That was an awful time for Alex, Delia.'

'Cordelia!' she said, correcting him.

'Yes—I'm sorry. Cordelia. Although I shall always think of you as Delia. Why didn't you tell us who you were?'

'There was no reason to.'

'Where are you heading for?'

'Home.'

'Not to Leeds?' he gasped incredulously.

'Yes. I have to see my parents.'

'But you're in no fit state to drive, let alone drive all the way to Leeds. I'll run you to the station, if you like.'

'No—thank you, James. I don't want to leave anything here, you see.'

James sighed, seeing her mind was made up. 'In that case, I'll take you.'

'No—you can't. How will you get back?'

'Train.'

'But—what about the hunt you were joining today?'

He grinned, cutting through her objections and climbing in behind the wheel of her car. 'There'll be another hunt tomorrow. Get in. We'll stop for petrol and something to eat on the way.'

Climbing in and closing the door, as James turned on the ignition and the car began to move off down the drive, Cordelia turned and saw Maxine standing on the steps of the hall, a rather forlorn figure. All that had to be said between them had been said and, feeling a hard lump rising in her throat, she smiled before lowering her head and wiping away the tears which began to run unheeded down her pale cheeks.'

'I'm awfully grateful to you, James,' she said when she was more composed. 'I have to admit that I really didn't feel up to driving to Leeds—but I had to get away from Stanfield before Alex returned.'

'Think nothing of it. I'm glad to be able to help. You know that. You're in love with Alex, aren't you?'

She nodded, swallowing hard. 'Yes. How did you know?'

'I'd have to be blind not to see it. He must be a damn fool for letting you go like this. I'll tell him so when I get back. I'm insanely jealous, you know,' he grinned. 'I had hoped to win you over myself.'

Fresh tears sprung to Cordelia's eyes and she threw him a grateful, appreciative look, for she knew he was only trying to lighten the situation in an attempt to make her feel better.

His gaze was soft when he glanced sideways at her and, reaching out, he squeezed her cold hands, placed quietly in her lap, in an effort to comfort her. She looked so wretched sitting there.

'Sorry. I know what you must be going through—but he's a lucky devil to have a girl like you crazy about him. Although—I suppose I can understand how much all this has upset him. He still suffers too much from those unpleasant memories to be able to dwell on them calmly. It was a frightful business when his wife died.'

'Did he love her?'

'No—at least not in the way I think you would interpret the word love. It wasn't her first affair, either.'

'Did Alex know?'

'Yes, but being away in France there was little he could do about it then.'

'What was she like?'

'Pamela? Oh—beautiful, glamorous—a typical society girl. Not really Alex's type at all. As you know he's a private man, whose preference is for quiet, unpretentious pleasures rather than the world of glamour.'

'However it may have looked at the time, James, my brother was not having an affair with Alex's wife. I knew him too well, you see. I cannot believe it of him. I never will. I just wish I had been able to find some way of convincing Alex.'

Sadly, when Cordelia looked at James's grim

profile, she could see he didn't believe her. She rested her head against the upholstery and closed her eyes, letting her thoughts drift back to Stanfield and Alex, unable to believe at that moment that the love they had shared for so brief a time was over.

Oh, Alex, Alex, her heart cried silently, remembering how wonderful it had felt to have him hold her, to kiss her. Before he had known her true identity she had been trying to determine a way so that her love and her career could go hand in hand. But in one day she had lost them both.

None of it was his doing. He was not the one who had deceived her. She was the guilty one. Shock over the whole horrendous affair had rendered her temporarily numb, but she knew that as it melted away it would give way to real suffering.

Whatever Billy's reasons had been for being at the same hotel as Alex's wife that night, when the Zeppelins had dropped their murderous bombs on London, she would not believe he was having an affair with her. There had to be another reason for him being there.

Her mind drifted back to the last time she had been at Edenthorpe, and her parents' shocked reaction when she had told them that Captain Alex Frankland was her employer.

She remembered how she had suspected then that something was wrong, a suspicion which had not been dispelled by their nervous explanation that the name reminded them of a Franklyn who had been in the same regiment as Billy, who had also been killed in France, and that the name brought back tragic memories of their son.

She remembered the unease she had felt on her return journey to Stanfield Hall, feeling there was a dark and terrible secret no one spoke of. But now she knew, when the familiar walls of her home loomed before her, that Edenthorpe had thrown its terrible secret up at last.

Lord and Lady Langhorne were surprised to see their daughter home—although somewhat alarmed when they saw the dressing on her face. James quickly told them that she had slightly injured herself taking a tumble from her horse during a hunt, reassuring them that apart from the cut on her face she would be all right.

James stayed for dinner and Lady Langhorne was both charmed and captivated by him. He was obviously a gentleman and, not surprisingly, she was curious as to the relationship between him and Cordelia, whose quietness since her return to Edenthorpe had not gone unnoticed.

It was only after James had departed for the station to catch the train to Norfolk, that she made it quite clear he was nothing more than a good friend. Ignoring the disappointment which clouded her mother's face, it was then that she told them of her reason for coming back to Edenthorpe.

She confronted them both, pale and afraid of what they would tell her. Now she was back at Edenthorpe she would have liked to believe that everything was the same as it had always been—but it wasn't and she could not go on pretending that it was. She had to know the truth about Billy.

'I know the truth about Billy,' she said quietly. 'Why did you tell me he was killed in France—when you knew he was killed during an air raid on London?'

Her parents were sitting side by side on the settee while she stood by the fire, too restless to sit down. A look of unease passed between them and they both seemed to grow much older as they faced their daughter, knowing the truth could no longer be kept from her.

'How much do you know?' asked her mother, looking distraught as well as confused.

Cordelia looked from one to the other accusingly. 'Lord Frankland discovered who I was. He told me. It was awful. Why did you let me go on believing he was killed in the war—when all the time his body was found with Lord Frankland's wife in a bombed-out hotel? You must have known I would find out one day.'

'We hoped and prayed you wouldn't,' said her father. 'You and Billy were always so special to each other and, knowing how much you worshipped him, we wanted to save you from the shameful circumstances of his death. Fortunately there was so much else going on at the time that it failed to make newspaper headlines. And it wasn't too difficult to keep the truth from you—you were in America at the time.'

'And David—and Georgina—and Emily? They all knew, I suppose?'

'Yes,' her mother said quietly. 'And they agreed to say nothing about it. We were thinking of you, Cordelia. We did it to protect you. You must believe that.'

Cordelia swallowed down the threatened tears and turned and looked into the low fire. 'I know. But you should have told me from the beginning. It would have saved me from so much pain. I would never have gone to work for Captain Frankland at Stanfield Hall had I known.'

Hearing a catch in her voice, her father rose and went to her, placing his hands on her shoulders and turning her to face him, the sadness he saw in her eyes wrenching his heart. At that moment she bore no resemblance to the independent young woman who had left Edenthorpe to devote all her time and energy to her career.

'Will you be returning to Stanfield Hall?'

She shook her head miserably. 'No,' she whispered. 'When he knew who I was, I believe he hated me.'

Her father searched her face with a steady,

understanding gaze. 'And you are in love with him, aren't you?'

She nodded, unable to keep her tears in check a minute longer. Her father folded her in his arms and tenderly stroked her hair, rocking her as he used to when she was a child as she sobbed quietly against his chest.

'Hush, Cordelia. You must not upset yourself so,' he murmured gently. 'I am sure Captain Frankland was angry and I can understand why—considering the circumstances. To discover that his secretary has deceived him as to her true identity must have been bad enough—but to find out you are the sister of the man he is so sure was having an affair with his wife must have come as a terrible blow. I don't wonder he was angry.

'But when people are angry they say things they don't mean. He'll calm down in time, you'll see—when the storm blows itself out.'

'No,' she mumbled. 'You don't know him.' Suddenly she lifted her head and looked up at her father. 'Do you believe Billy was having an affair with his wife?'

Her father released her, shaking his head sadly. 'I don't know. All the evidence suggests that he was and yet—well—I have never believed it in my heart.'

'And you, Mother? Do you?'

'No. I never have. He was incapable of indulging in a sordid affair—especially as he was engaged to Abigail—such a lovely girl. But how could we prove otherwise?'

'What was he like on his last leave? Was he afraid of returning to the front?'

'Not really,' her father answered. 'He knew he had to, you see.'

'He and Abigail had spent a lovely two weeks together,' said her mother, her face white and strained, 'talking of how they would be married the moment the War was over. When she heard of his death—and the manner in which he had died, she was devastated and confused by it. But she was convinced of his love and refused to believe what he was accused of.

'The day he left Edenthorpe, he was to travel to London to meet up with his friend, a fellow officer in his regiment who had also been on leave. They were to return to France together.'

Cordelia looked at her mother sharply, for a tiny hint of a suspicion was beginning to form in her mind. She was almost too afraid to ask the next question for she was certain she already knew the answer. 'What was the name of this fellow officer Billy was supposed to meet, Mother? Do you remember?'

'Why, yes. Billy brought him home on occasion. He was a charmer, as I remember, and quite taken with Emily. Very good on the piano, too. His name was Michael. Michael Martin.'

The name rendered Cordelia speechless and she stared at her mother as if turned to stone.

'Why, what is it, dear?' she said with concern. 'Is anything the matter? You look so strange all of a sudden. Does the name mean anything to you?'

Cordelia nodded, remembering the letters she had found which had fallen out of a drawer in the attic, on the day she had been sorting out some furniture which was to be sold. They had been love letters—written to Pamela, Alex's wife, and signed Michael. Suddenly her face became alight with hope that at last she had stumbled upon something that would help to clear Billy' name.

'Do you remember where Billy was to meet Michael Martin?' she asked eagerly.

'No, I don't remember him saying. Do you, dear?' she asked her husband, who shook his head in answer. 'Why? Is it important?'

'Yes. You see, I believe it was Michael who was having the affair with Lord Frankland's wife—and that Billy had gone to the hotel to meet him there.'

Her parents gasped. 'But how can you know that?' asked her father. 'Billy's was the only body apart from Lord Frankland's wife that was found in the rubble.'

'I suppose it is possible that others in the hotel at the time escaped the blast,' said her mother thoughtfully. 'But what makes you suspect Michael?'

'Because one day, quite by chance, I happened to come across some letters addressed to Pamela, Lord Frankland's wife—love letters—from someone called Michael. Now do you see why I suspect him—and that Billy had gone to the hotel to meet him. It's all too much of a coincidence, don't you think?'

'It certainly appears that way,' said her father, at last beginning to understand what his daughter was getting at. 'But what did you do with the letters? Did you give them to Lord Frankland?'

'No.' She sighed deeply. 'I did not wish to cause him unnecessary suffering, for there was every possibility he knew nothing of his wife's infidelity. I gave them to Maxine—his aunt.'

'Then surely if she were to show them to Captain Frankland he would begin to look at all this in a new light,' said her mother hopefully, her expression of anguish beginning to fade a little. 'Perhaps you could telephone her and explain it all.'

Cordelia shook her head. 'No. I would rather see her. She was very upset when I left, and if she has to confront her nephew with this, then I think it best if I am with her.'

'Will you be all right?' asked her father with some concern for her well being. 'Would you like me to accompany you?'

'No, thank you, Father. This is something I must do myself. But I can't tell you what it means that, after all that has happened, at last I have this one thing to hold on to.'

When Alex returned to Stanfield Hall, one hour after Cordelia's departure with James, it did not surprise him to find her gone. He could not bring himself to follow her.

In the days following her departure his rage showed through and, in his black mood, the staff at Stanfield avoided him. Only Maxine understood what he was going through; being aware of his deep love for Cordelia, she was afraid this latest blow would destroy him. Everything reminded him of her. He could not banish her from his heart and mind. Even her horse, the gentle mare she always rode, stared with huge, forlorn eyes out of its box.

It was two weeks after she had left when Maxine received a call from Cordelia, saying there was something of the utmost importance she had to see her about. She had waited two weeks in the hope that Diana would have left. Maxine collected her from the station and took her back to Stanfield Hall.

'Now, what is it that is so important to bring you back to Stanfield?' she asked when they were together in the drawing-room.

'The letters, Maxine. Pamela's letters I found in the attic. You must show them to Alex. You see—I believe the Michael she was seeing was my brother's friend—a fellow officer in the same regiment. On the night of the air raid, Billy was supposed to meet Michael somewhere in London and they were to return to France together. Oh, Maxine, don't you see? They must have arranged to meet at the hotel. It's the only reason I can think of for him being there. Will you show Alex the letters?'

Suddenly Maxine looked quite distraught. 'I can't show him the letters, Cordelia.'

'You—you can't? But why?'

'I destroyed them.'

Cordelia stared at her in disbelief. 'Oh, Maxine—no. I was relying on those letters to help clear Billy's name. Why did you destroy them?'

'I could see no point in holding onto them. I wanted to save him from further pain, you see. It was a part of his life that was over and done with—or so I thought at the time. But now—I wish I'd kept them.'

Cordelia sighed, not wishing to dwell on them, for Maxine was clearly upset by what she had done. 'Oh, well—just as long as Alex knows they existed. If we both tell him about them then maybe we can convince him of Billy's innocence. How is Alex, Maxine?'

'Oh—I don't think he's as bad as he was. The

black mood that descended on him after you left has abated somewhat—at least the staff no longer keep their distance. He's still difficult—nigh impossible at times, I would say, but he misses you, Cordelia. That I do know.'

'And I miss him, Maxine. He'll never know just how much.'

They both turned, for at that moment the door opened and Alex stepped into the room.

Chapter Eleven

Cordelia got slowly to her feet and stared across the room at Alex, momentarily forgetful of the reason that had brought her to Stanfield. A wave of happiness swept over her as she was able to look once again on those features buried so deep in her heart. His face was drawn, his mouth held in a tight line, and she was conscious of a curious feeling of tenderness at the stray lock of hair that insisted on falling over his brow.

However, his stony countenance told her that, whatever she had hoped, he had not forgiven her for her deception, nor could he ever forget who she was. There was to be no reconciliation, no further embraces or past differences forgotten. There was no welcoming smile, nothing at that moment to indicate he still cared. Managing to subdue her disappointment, she pulled herself together.

'Hello, Alex,' she said quietly. 'You knew I was coming?'

Entering the room, Alex had seen her at once and his breath froze within his chest. She was still as lovely, achingly, tormentingly so. Her face still bore the marks of the fall—a slight bruising and a scar that would go with time, but it did nothing to mar her loveliness.

'Yes. Maxine told me to expect a visit from you.'

As he moved towards her, Cordelia could see, as his grey eyes studied her, that, despite the harshness of his features, there was something about his expression that told her he was pleased to see her. There was a flickering of admiration in his eyes—and love, which filled her with a wonderful elation.

But it was gone almost as soon as it had appeared, for when he stood before her his grey eyes remained fixed on hers without a smile to soften his expression. 'How are you? Fully recovered from your fall, I hope?'

Alex now knew Cordelia had not been lying when she had told him she suspected Diana had been responsible for the incident by over-riding her. After talking to several people who had been at the back of the hunting field that day, they had confirmed this. Aware of the width and depth of the ditch she had fallen into, he knew she could have been seriously injured—or worse. She could have been killed.

He had left Diana in no doubt of his deep displeasure over the unfortunate incident before she had left Stanfield with James—although she had coolly denied having anything to do with it. However, Alex was inclined to believe Cordelia's side of the story over anything Diana had to say on the matter.

'Yes—thank you,' Cordelia replied. 'And you?'

He ignored her question and moved a little closer to her, his eyes hard and fixed firmly on her face.

'Enough of civilities, Cordelia. What are you doing here? I thought everything had been said between us. To disappear so suddenly and then reappear out of the blue like this, leads me to think it must be something of the utmost importance to bring you back.'

'It is, but you could have refused to see me.'

No, he thought, how could he? The chance of seeing her once more was too much for him to resist.

Maxine made a move to get up out of her chair. 'I'm sure you would prefer it if I weren't here. I'll go and leave you alone.'

'No,' said Cordelia in alarm. 'Please don't go, Maxine.'

A faint smile curled Alex's lips, so faint it was

barely discernible. 'Why—what's this? Are you afraid of being alone with me?'

'No—of course not. Only I need Maxine here to verify what I have to say.'

'Really?' he said with deep irony, raising his eyebrows and looking from one to the other. 'What is this? A conspiracy?'

'You must know why I'm here, Alex. After what you revealed to me about my brother before I left Stanfield, you did not think I would let it lie and just ignore it, did you?'

A flash of anger in Alex's eyes told Cordelia she might have gone too far, but she had to go on for Billy's sake and her parents'. But she must remain calm—the success of her mission depended on it.

'I do not wish to discuss it,' said Alex coldly.

'But I have to,' Cordelia persisted. 'I know you must have suffered greatly—but so have my parents.'

'What are you trying to say?'

'That it was not my brother your wife was meeting that day.'

'Oh! And you know, of course?'

Cordelia detected the hint of sarcasm in his tone but chose to ignore it. 'No—not for certain, but I strongly suspect it was his friend.'

'Who was?'

'A fellow officer by the name of Michael Martin. They had both been home on leave and were supposed to meet up that day and return to France together.'

'I see. And why was this Michael Martin's body not found in the rubble of the hotel—along with that of my wife and your brother?'

'I don't know.'

'No. And you never will. It is highly commendable that you should want to clear your brother's name—but why should you suspect this Michael Martin of being my wife's lover?'

Drawing a deep breath, quickly Cordelia told him about the letters she had found, how she had begun to read them before realising what they were.

Alex was watching her with an icy calm, his face set in stiff lines. 'And what were they?'

'Love letters—to—to your wife from someone called Michael.'

'I see. And where are these letters now?'

'I—I gave them to Maxine.'

'Wouldn't it have been more sensible to give them to me?'

'I couldn't. If you knew nothing of the affair, then it would only have caused you unnecessary grief.'

'Thank you,' he said with irony. 'How very obliging of you. Where are they now, Maxine?'

'I destroyed them.'

If Alex was perturbed by this, he did not show it.

'I see. Why did you destroy them?'

'I'm sorry. I realise now that I shouldn't have. At the time I believed the affair was over and done with. I believed nothing could be gained by holding onto them.'

He nodded, fixing his face once more on Cordelia. 'There is something I think I should tell you. You see, what you perhaps don't know about my late wife is that she had several lovers. Your brother was not the first.'

His tone was mocking, making Cordelia's mission here today seem trivial, but unknown to him James had already told her this.

'My brother was not having an affair with your wife,' she said quietly and desperately. 'Please—you must believe that. How can I convince you?'

'I'm sorry, but you cannot convince me of his innocence. I'm not insensitive to what your parents must have suffered—and I respect your attempt to do all you can to clear your brother's name—but you cannot ask me to believe this without more proof.'

He continued to look at her, his face hard as were his grey eyes. Defeated, Cordelia sighed.

'Very well. Then there is nothing more to be said.'

'No.'

Maxine slipped out of the room, leaving them alone while she went to fetch her car to take Cordelia back to the station. Alex spoke as

Cordelia picked up her bag and was about to follow her.

'What will you do now?'

She lowered her eyes, unable to look into his, which were so cold. His voice was flat and terse, as if he were addressing a stranger. 'Return to London and seek another position.'

Alex's manner softened a little. 'Despite what has occurred between us—and whatever the truth of the matter—I do wish you every success with your career, knowing how important it is to you. Should you want a reference, then do not hesitate to ask.'

'Thank you.' Slowly she moved towards the door where she paused, the pain of parting from him almost too much to bear. 'Tell me, Alex,' she said, turning to face him, her whole heart in her eyes. 'Have you made up your mind to dislike me all your life?'

Her words, spoken with such quiet, caused Alex to stand quite still and look at her. His face was taut with emotion and within his eyes something moved and glowed a little, giving an indication of a softening to his attitude.

Cordelia's face was very white; her eyes, locked with his, unwavering, were diamond bright with unshed tears. The sight was almost beyond his bearing. Unable to resist the soft bewitchment of those imploring eyes, he strode towards her and stood looking down at her upturned face, wanting to touch her but afraid of the consequences of doing so.

'Dislike? I don't dislike you, Cordelia. Never think that. You know what my feelings are. I think I made them plain to you that night in the music room when I found you playing Chopin on the piano. The memory of that will remain with me always.'

'And you have no wish to refresh that memory?'

'Dear Lord, stop it, Cordelia,' he said hoarsely. 'My arms ache to hold you—but you must see that grim reality prevents us from becoming further involved with each other. Dear Lord, I'll miss you, but we can't go back. Both of us know that.'

The tears spilled over Cordelia's lashes as she turned resolutely away from him, but she experienced a feeling of absolute joy in knowing he still cared, he still loved her. 'Then you must forget you ever met me. Goodbye, Alex. I think Maxine is waiting.'

Alex stood there a long time after she had gone, feeling the chill of her leaving. Never, in all his life, had he felt as wretched as he did at that moment.

Cordelia didn't turn and look back as Maxine drove her to the station, but it seemed as if her heart would break. She blinked back her tears, refusing to give in to anguish. No doubt time, determination and hard work would help her, for she must keep her sights fixed on clearing Billy's name. She would start by finding Michael Martin—if he hadn't been killed in the War.

'I will try and talk to Alex, Cordelia,' said Maxine, breaking in on her thoughts. 'I do promise. But you can see how he is. However, he loves you. That I do know.'

'Apparently not enough,' Cordelia replied sadly.

Cordelia would probably never see Alex again, she knew that now. Whatever illusions she might have had where he was concerned were gone. But she missed him horribly. Time did nothing to lessen her heartache and the part of her he had awoken had shrivelled away and died. The days she could cope with, for she had things to do to keep her mind occupied, but the nights were agony.

She returned to the flat in London that she shared with Kitty and, although her parting from Stanfield and trying to discover what had happened to Michael Martin was uppermost in her mind at this time, she knew she would have to start thinking about her immediate future, for her career was still very important to her—perhaps more so now she knew she had to put Alex from her mind. To embark on something new would be good for her.

It was her father who first gave her the idea of going to America to work, thinking it might not be a bad thing for her to get away from her recent problems—and her obsession over Billy's death. He had been in contact with some close family friends—the Merlins in New York. Cordelia had been staying with them at their home on Long Island at the time of Billy's death.

Since before the War the Merlins had begun to embrace the world of art. Two of the sons had studied art in Paris and, on returning to New York as accomplished artists, they had founded a gallery to sell their work. One of the brothers, with a keen eye on the future, and recognising the profits to be made from the creative eruptions in the world of art, had opened an auction house in New York. Upon hearing from Lord Langhorne that Cordelia was seeking employment, he had offered her a position with the firm.

Cordelia was grateful for the offer and promised to think it over carefully before making a decision. She had to admit that, having a love of art, the position did appeal to her—and besides, she was keen to get on with her future which, if she accepted the offer, seemed well formulated—but first she had to find Michael Martin.

As the daylight hours became shorter and winter descended on London, Kitty did her best to dispel Cordelia's mood of melancholy. Once again she began to integrate herself in their wide circle of amusing and entertaining friends—smart, rich and aristocratic—visiting the theatre or the ballet at Sadler's Wells, going on to the Savoy afterwards or to some other fashionable rendezvous to dance the night away to the latest tunes, the music of Irving Berlin and George Gershwin being extremely popular.

Meanwhile, Cordelia telephoned the headquarters of the King's Own Yorkshire Light Infantry in York, which had been both Billy's and Michael Martin's regiment. It was with absolute relief that she was told Michael Martin had survived the War—although he had suffered an injury which had resulted in the loss of one of his legs.

After demobilisation they had lost track of him. However, they gave her his home address in Darlington, so she did have something to go on. If he no longer lived there, then members of his family might know where he had gone. She telephoned her father and gave him the information. He promised to see into the matter himself to save her the trouble of going all the way up to Darlington. He would let her know what transpired.

Feeling they were getting somewhere at last in solving the mystery of Billy's last day in London, Cordelia's spirits began to rise. She even came to a decision regarding her future and wrote to the Merlins in New York, informing them that she would be more than happy to accept their offer of a position with the 'House of Merlin', and she would await a letter from them informing her when they would like her to be in New York.

Happier than she had felt in a long time, she went with Kitty to a celebratory birthday party at the Embassy Club in Old Bond Street—well known for its presentation of sophisticated cabaret and a popular meeting place for the rich and famous. It was patronised by the Prince of Wales and his friends, who were considered to be the pace-setters among upper-class society—food for the writers of the glossy magazines.

The atmosphere inside the club, with its elegant décor, was warm and intimate and in full swing, the hour being close to midnight, with tables and chairs arranged with a skilful casualness, at which men and women sat about drinking and talking. Others danced on the small, crowded dance floor to the band playing the sentimental music of the hour. The soft light showed the sylph-like forms of the ladies, with snowy shoulders and pink flushed faces.

Cordelia was feeling relaxed and just leaving the dance floor with Jeremy when suddenly she saw Alex coming towards her, lean and immaculate, in a black evening suit. Unable to believe that joy could be so great, she stopped while Jeremy, believing she was still following him, went back to their table to join the others, who were becoming increasingly boisterous as the evening wore on.

Cordelia stared at Alex in shocked surprise, at a complete loss for words when he stood before her, looking down, his glorious grey eyes locked on hers, which shone with a heart-stopping brilliance.

Their meeting was as much a surprise to Alex as it was to Cordelia. His eyes roamed involuntarily over the length of her body in appraisal, for she was dressed in a diaphanous chiffon evening-dress, worn with a long scarf and a spray of orchids on her shoulder, very thin wrist chains and bracelets encircling her bare arms. There was a rather wistful air of melancholy about her that, besides giving her an alluring quality, also made one feel protective towards her.

During all the weeks Cordelia had been without Alex, she had done nothing but think of him; now they were face to face, all she could do was stare at him, feeling painfully self-conscious, not knowing what to say and waiting for him to speak.

'Hello, Cordelia. You look sensational.'

The tone in which it was said brought a warm glow to her cheeks and her voice trembled a little when she spoke.

'Thank you. How are you, Alex?'

'Very well. I'm in London for a couple of days to try and talk Lord Curzon's son-in-law into selling me one of his horses.'

Cordelia knew it was Fruity Metcalf he spoke of, who was a close associate of the Prince of Wales.

'Somehow he talked me into coming here,' Alex continued. 'I know the Price of Wales patronises this place and is expected to arrive with a party around midnight. I've been invited to join them, but I'm beginning to wish I'd declined the invitation.'

Cordelia smiled, 'Anyone would be honoured to meet the Prince—but I can see you don't like it here very much, do you?' she said, noting his look of distaste as two young revellers pushed past him.

'Nightclubs are not my favourite places,' he said softly. 'I prefer somewhere with a quieter, more intimate atmosphere. Look—would you like to join me—if your friends don't mind, that is? We'll ask Luigi to find us a table somewhere less crowded.'

'Yes,' she replied, almost shyly. 'I'd like that.'

The Embassy was run by Luigi, an Italian restaurateur, who was noted for his discretion, knowing the likes and dislikes of his distinguished clientele. He immediately looked for a table where Captain Frankland and the lady could be more private.

Ignoring the inquiring, humorous glances thrown at them from her friends, Cordelia allowed Alex to lead her to the empty table in a corner, where champagne was brought and poured by a waiter, the remainder left in the bottle in a silver ice bucket at the side of their table.

Alex looked across at her, thinking how poised she looked, how elegant in such an expensive and fashionable establishment. For Miss King to patronise the Embassy Club would have been out of the question—but for Cordelia Hamilton-King it was quite another matter.

'It is evident that you are quite at home mixing with the coroneted lords and ladies of society, Cordelia.'

'Considering my father is one of them, it is hardly surprising,' she replied with a smile.

'Your friends seem in a boisterous mood. Is it an occasion that brings you here tonight?'

'Yes. A birthday party.'

'I see. Not yours, of course. I seem to remember that your birthday is in August.'

Cordelia flushed, unconsciously raising her hand to her neck and fingering the gold cross he had bought her in Cambridge. He noticed and smiled.

'Yes,' she replied. 'I'm flattered that you should remember.'

'How could I ever forget? It makes me happy to see that you still wear my gift.'

Cordelia lowered her eyes beneath his disturbing gaze as memories of that wonderful day they'd spent together came flooding back.

'H-how is Maxine?' she asked after a brief silence.

'Quite well—apart from her rheumatism, which always troubles her at the onset of winter.'

'I'm sorry to hear that. And the colt—the one you bought from Newmarket?'

'He's doing well.' He fell silent, looking at her closely, for the first time in his life horses being the last thing he wanted to talk about.

The light in the Club was muted and when he looked at her her eyes were large and dark in her lovely face. Her hand, slender and white, was resting on the table, toying with the stem of her wine glass. How he would like to reach out and take it in his own. 'Tell me what you've been doing, Cordelia. You never did write, asking me for a reference.'

'No. I haven't needed to.'

'So—what happened to the career which was so important to you?'

'It still is. I'm considering going to America. I've had an offer to work in New York.'

Cordelia didn't see Alex's eyes cloud over when she said this.

'I see. What kind of work is it?'

'I'm not sure yet—although it does sound interesting. Some friends of my family are very much involved in the art world. Two of them, having studied art in Paris, are accomplished artists themselves and have founded a gallery in New

York to sell their work. Recently they opened some auction rooms and have offered me a position there.'

'And will you take it?'

Leaning back in his chair with his long fingers entwined in front of him, Alex was studying her closely, calm and relaxed, as if he was waiting for more than her answer to his question. Cordelia met his gaze directly and nodded, picking up her glass and taking a sip of champagne. With something of an effort she answered his question.

'Yes—I already have.'

He nodded slowly. 'I see. And when do you leave for New York?'

'I don't know exactly. Shortly after Christmas, I think.'

'Then I wish you every success. The next time I'm thinking of buying some paintings for Stanfield, I'll know where to go.' He rose suddenly when the music became low and sentimental, taking the glass from her fingers and setting it aside. 'Come. Let's dance. The floor isn't as crowded as it was.'

Taking her hand he led her out onto the dance floor, drawing her to him, his hand coming to rest firmly on her waist. She sighed and melted against him, giving herself entirely to the magic of the music and the joy of being in his arms.

He danced well. Despite his leg wound, sustained during the War, there was little sign of his limp as he guided her slowly around the floor, his eyes fixed intently on hers, the music and his closeness filling her with warmth. The wealth of emotions his nearness induced in her almost overwhelmed her and she wondered if he could feel the beating of her heart.

Time seemed meaningless and Cordelia was aware of nothing in the world except this man and this moment. Neither wanted the music to end. After the first dance they danced a second and then a third, neither of them speaking, grateful to Ambrose, the bandleader, for not changing the tempo of the music. Gradually Alex's hand drew her closer and he placed his cheek against her hair.

With her head resting on his shoulder and her eyes closed, Cordelia caught the familiar smell of his cologne, and felt the hardness of his body pressed close to hers as they moved in unison, completely attuned to each other.

It could have been a day, a month or a year later when the music stopped. Lifting her head, Cordelia opened her eyes and saw his head poised over hers. There was no need for words as they stood in their enchanted circle and looked into each other's eyes, aware of nothing and no one but each other. But then Kitty was beside them, breaking the magic of the moment. Unconsciously, still holding Alex's hand, Cordelia turned and looked at her.

'I'm sorry to interrupt, Cordelia, but we're leaving. Alfred would like us all to go to his place for a bit of a party. Are you coming with us?'

'Er—I don't know. Kitty—this is Captain Frankland—you remember—I used to work for him.'

Kitty stared at him boldly and smiled broadly. 'Yes, I know. We met at Ascot—although we were not introduced at the time. We were in a spot of bother over spraying champagne all over the place. Do you remember, Captain Frankland?'

He laughed, his white teeth gleaming in the subdued lighting. 'I doubt I shall ever forget it, Miss—'

'Wyatt—but Kitty will do.' She smiled, charmed by him, understanding perfectly why it was so difficult for Cordelia to get him out of her system. Although, if tonight was anything to go by, it seemed she never would. It had been noticed and remarked upon that they'd only had eyes for each other ever since Captain Frankland had arrived. 'Well, Cordelia? Are you coming?'

Feeling Alex gently squeeze her hand, she thought it was his way of telling her not to go—and she was just as reluctant to part from him now.

'No, Kitty. I'll stay.'

'How will you get home?'

'I'll see she gets home safely,' said Alex.

Kitty eyes danced mischievously from one to

the other. 'Yes, I'm sure you will. Oh, I'll be staying at Alfred's, by the way—so don't wait up, will you?'

'I won't. Enjoy the party.'

The music was starting up again as she turned back to Alex and they danced some more. When it ended and they drew apart, she smiled up at him, a smile that almost stopped his heart.

'Shall we sit down?' he asked softly.

She shook her head.

'Wouldn't you like some more champagne?'

'No. I think I've drunk enough for one evening.'

'Would you like to leave?'

'Yes. I think I'd like that—but—what about your friends?'

'Oh—they'll hardly notice I've gone once the Prince of Wales arrives. Wouldn't you like to stay and meet him?'

'No.'

'Good. Neither would I. Come along—let's see about getting your coat.'

The night was cold, the gas lamps casting a yellow glow along the streets. Piccadilly Circus was a flashing and twinkling multitude of lights, movement and colour and was humming like a beehive as the theatres and music-halls emptied themselves onto the streets.

Huddled in the warmth of her coat, Cordelia relaxed beside Alex in his car, thinking back to the first time they had met as they turned the corner off Oxford Street, the very place where they'd almost collided, and she smiled. Turning, Alex gave her a meaningful look, also remembering the incident, and he smiled, but neither of them mentioned it.

Pulling up outside the building in which Cordelia lived, Alex climbed out of the car and went round and opened the door for her. She stepped out, moving towards the short flight of steps leading up to the door, stopping suddenly and looking up at him. The lines of his face were etched like granite in the starlight.

'Can I offer you some coffee?'

Alex looked at her for a long time before answering. His grey eyes, almost as black as his sleek hair in the darkness of the street, were intently studying her face, bathed in the soft silvery glow from the moon. She was so poised, so still.

'That is not what I want, Cordelia. I think we both know that. If you let me inside then I think we both know what will happen—even though there can never be anything more between us. Is that what you want?'

There was more eloquence in Cordelia's silence than any words she could have uttered. Her head told her to go inside alone, but her heart was telling her something else. She knew she was going to listen to her heart for she was certain she was destined to love this man. She knew that what they were about to embark on was dangerous folly, but what she felt for him was too strong to resist any longer—too strong, too compelling for either of them to resist.

Lowering her eyes, Cordelia unlocked the door and went inside.

Not wanting the strong, dangerous current of attraction that had been flowing between them all evening to be broken—or perhaps it was his own desire, his own desperate need to possess this woman he had desired and loved ever since he had first set eyes on her—Alex hesitated for just a moment before following her.

Chapter Twelve

The flat Cordelia and Kitty shared was large enough for entertaining a few friends, yet small enough to give a feeling of cosy intimacy—as it did now when Alex came to stand behind Cordelia, slipping her coat from her shoulders. They did not turn on any lights for the starlight, entering through the windows, bathed the rooms in a soft, silvery sheen.

Cordelia stood quite still, waiting for what would happen, expectant, hopeful. Alex's hands stroked her shoulders and she could feel the warmth of his breath on her flesh as he lowered his head and placed his lips in the warm, scented hollow of her neck where a pulse fluttered beneath her skin.

She closed her eyes and melted back into his arms as they wrapped themselves around her. Slowly he turned her round to face him, his arm tightening around her waist until her body was moulded against his. In his eyes, which looked down at her face, tilted up to his, were all the things he wanted to say yet remained unspoken.

Slowly he lowered his head and covered her mouth with his own. Her lips warmed under his, parted and softened, her sweet breath sighing through. After a time, which seemed like an eternity, he raised his head just a little.

'Are you sure about this, Cordelia?' he murmured, his lips close to hers. 'Are you sure this is what you want?'

'Yes,' she whispered. 'Oh, yes,' and, slipping her arms around his neck, she drew his face down to hers. It was too late to turn back now—much too late, and she didn't want to. She wanted more than his kisses and she felt in him the same need—urgent—demanding to be satisfied.

Placing his arm beneath her knees, Alex scooped her up into his arms and carried her into her bedroom, standing her on the carpet and slipping her dress off her shoulders. Neither of them knew how they divested themselves of their clothing; as Cordelia stepped out of her dress, it lay like a shimmering pool on the floor.

When she stood naked before him, there was no shame or modesty and Alex looked at her with awe. Her body was so slender, so supple—he was almost afraid of its perfection. Drawing her down onto the bed, he at last took her into his arms.

Pulling her close, he kissed her flesh, satin smooth beneath his lips, causing a multitude of sensations to explode inside her. The texture of his skin next to hers was smooth and warm. He was sure of himself, his hands subtly experienced, caressing, exploring, arousing her to the pitch where love becomes irresistible.

His kisses were long, and those, too, were strangely skilled. He led her gently into the knowledge of lovemaking, arousing a passion inside her that made her almost afraid of its intensity—an intensity she did not understand.

Cordelia's senses soared as she was swept along on long shuddering waves of pleasure—mounting—overwhelming her, until it became almost unbearable. She arched her spine and pressed her breasts to his bare chest, feeling the urgency in his hard, lean body. At last she yielded her body to his, which was bursting with power and force. They became like two vines wrapped around each other—united in an indulgence of love and violent pleasure until, at last, there was the ultimate, wonderful release.

They dozed and made love again, leisurely now, their skin warm and moist, glistening with perspiration, until they were gloriously fulfilled. It was wonderful. It felt so right between them. Finally they slept, their bodies entwined.

* * *

Strong winter sunshine spilled through the windows and over the bed. It was late when Cordelia awoke and stretched in blissful lassitude, feeling like a flower opening to the sun's warmth. She opened her eyes, remembering the night, and she was filled with a blazing happiness.

She turned, expecting to see Alex still lying there beside her, but the bed was empty. She snuggled into the hollow made by his body, feeling again the touch of him and her body tingled anew. She breathed deeply of the smell of his pine-scented cologne, which still lingered on the sheets, and closed her eyes.

Sounds from the kitchen disturbed her and, impatient to see Alex, she rose, draping a sheet about her naked body. Pushing open the kitchen door she expected to see him—but it was Kitty, having just returned from Alfred's party. Alex had gone.

She went back into her room and stood looking down into the square below. Even though he had gone she had a curiously calm and physical feeling of well-being.

When her eyes came to rest on the photograph of Billy, dressed in his military uniform, she remembered that during the whole night neither of them had mentioned him, and she realised it was because neither had wanted to spoil what they knew was inevitably going to happen between them. He had told her that nothing could come of it, but, nevertheless, no matter what happened, no one could undo the night they had shared.

But, even so, a small voice at the back of her mind mourned its passing and its wonder. Because of Alex's stubborn masculine pride and his refusal to put the past behind him—his inability to disregard the fact that Billy was her brother—there would be no more nights like that. But when he was faced with the truth—that Billy had been in the same hotel as his wife merely to meet his friend—what would he do then?

She missed him dreadfully and inwardly prayed he would phone her. She tried to reconcile in her mind his evident desire for her yet his reluctance to form any kind of relationship, but as the days passed she became hurt that he made no contact. Eventually she began to doubt his love, thinking, bleakly, that it hadn't been love at all. Perhaps that one night they had spent together had meant nothing more to him than a slaking of his desire.

Finally, she began to feel angry that she had been so foolish as to give herself to a man so hard and unfeeling. Had he merely been deceiving her? If that were so, then she would make certain she was never deceived again.

While Cordelia was gazing down into the square on the morning after Alex had left her, he was driving out of London, returning to Stanfield. He had risen when it was scarcely light and dressed, quietly looking down at Cordelia, his heart contracting with longing and pain on seeing how lovely she looked, bathed in the early morning glow.

She was still sleeping, her sweet curving form curled up among the tangled bedclothes, her head cushioned on her cap of thick golden hair. Her lips were moist and slightly parted, through which she breathed softly. One long slender leg was stretched out, incredibly perfect.

He almost weakened, feeling that he couldn't leave her, but then he saw the face of her brother, looking out at him from the photograph on her dressing-table, almost a mirror-image of Cordelia, and it was like having a bucket of cold water thrown over him. Pain tore through him—not the crippling pain from a wound, but the kind you could not see, the kind that had no location.

The betrayal and all the sickening humiliations heaped on him by his dead wife came flooding back in a multitude of different ways. Cordelia had had nothing to do with any of that, but how could he make her a part of his life when every time he looked at her he would see the face of her brother?

He left her then while he still had the strength to—before he weakened and laid down beside her once more—cursing the day she had come to Stanfield and into his life. The fact that she had concealed her true identity, and that William

Hamilton-King was her brother, was like a double profanation in itself.

But, he thought, his mood softening when his thoughts drifted back to their night of love, and how much pleasure they had derived from each other, now she had become a part of him. How could he ever live without her? But he would have to.

Even if it was proved that her brother had not been his wife's lover and, as Cordelia believed, he had been at the same hotel as his wife for some other reason—which he himself doubted—he could not ask her to abandon her career in America, which he knew was extremely important to her, for life at Stanfield.

It was three weeks later when Cordelia heard from her father, telling her that he had been to the address she had given him in Darlington, where Michael Martin's mother still lived. Michael no longer lived there, having moved to London after the war to become a pianist in a nightclub in Soho called the Pink Pussy Cat.

Cordelia could not believe he was so close, though she did not relish the thought of going there alone. This was where Jeremy came in handy. When asked if he would escort her, he happily agreed to do so, the prospect of spending any time with her at all too much to resist.

They went in search of the Pink Pussy Cat one

night, when the nightclubs were open. It was not the first occasion Cordelia had been to Soho, which was famous for its drinking clubs—a pleasure-seeking, licentious cosmopolitan quarter of London, which had added to the capital's flavour for the past three centuries. With friends she had often dined at some of the restaurants—Greek, Italian or French—which were a gastronomic delight.

The streets were crowded when they asked directions to the Pink Pussy Cat. They were told to go down a passage way on the right at the end of the street. The club they were looking for could be located at the end.

Passing lighted entrances and pictures on billboards portraying the entertainment on offer within, they eventually found the passageway, making their way along until they came to a dark corner at the end and saw a doorway with a sign above displaying the rather weathered figure of a pink cat.

Cordelia hesitated for a moment, reluctant to enter and descend the flight of stairs. A cold shiver ran down her spine, for it provoked a picture of how descending into Hades must look—the underworld abode for the souls of the dead. Even Jeremy was reluctant to enter.

'Are you quite certain you want to go down there?' he asked, not at all sure of what they were letting themselves in for. In no way did it resemble the more fashionable sort of clubs they were used to frequenting.

Cordelia nodded. 'I have to. I've told you how important it is that I see the man my father told me plays the piano here. I don't know his address so I have no alternative but to see him here.' At that moment music floated up to them from below as someone rattled out a popular number on piano keys.

She took a deep, decisive breath. 'Come along, Jeremy. It shouldn't take long and then,' she said, bestowing on him her most charming smile and squeezing his hand, 'you can take me for a meal at that lovely Italian restaurant we passed earlier.'

Unable to resist the opportunity of spending time with her alone, in a secluded corner of a nice little Italian restaurant along Greek Street, Jeremy immediately began descending the narrow flight of stairs to the basement. The commissionaire gave Cordelia a sly look out of the corner of his eyes, clearly wondering if she was one of the street women who hung around the doors waiting to accost patrons on their way home. Deciding she didn't look the type, he let them in.

The club was ill lit and damp, just one of the regular, sleazy haunts for people from all walks of life—one which was often raided by the police, they had been told before they came. Waiters hovered and scantily clad girls sat around on stools, smoking cigarettes protruding out of long holders.

The atmosphere was seedy, the clientele of an eccentric, dubious nature, which caused an involuntarily shudder to pass through Cordelia. She would be glad when she was back outside. Glancing around, through the haze of tobacco smoke she looked at the pianist, hoping it was Michael Martin. The waiter who brought them a drink confirmed that it was.

'Is it possible for me to speak to him?' Cordelia asked, experiencing a glorious feeling of relief at having found him at last.

The waiter glanced at a clock above the bar. 'He'll be taking a break in fifteen minutes. I'll tell him you want a word.'

'Thank you.'

The waiter went over to the piano and, after speaking close to his ear, Michael Martin curiously glanced their way, giving them a crooked smile.

When he eventually joined them at their table, Cordelia noticed his awkward gait, reminding her that he had lost a leg during the War. The waiter came and placed a large whisky in front of him. He was good looking, in a rugged kind of way, with curly brown hair and a charismatic smile.

He looked from Jeremy to Cordelia, waiting for one of them to speak, curious as to what it was they wanted. They certainly didn't fit the description of the usual motley crowd that patronised the

Pink Pussy Cat night after night. Their dress and manner were more in keeping with the kind of nightclubs catering for the upper classes.

'I'm Cordelia Hamilton-King,' said Cordelia by way of introduction, 'and this is a friend of mine, Jeremy Bingham. He kindly agreed to accompany me here tonight. I believe you were a friend of my brother Billy, Mr Martin?'

His eyes opened wide in amazement. 'Yes. We were in the same regiment and fought together in France. It was a terrible shock to learn of his death. Billy and I always got on well. You'd think that with so many of one's friends getting killed you would get used to it—but you never did. I was one of the lucky ones—despite losing a leg.'

'Yes. I'm sorry,' she replied, thinking that Mr Martin seemed like a well-mannered, articulate gentleman, slightly out of place in this undesirable nightclub.

'I'm happy to make your acquaintance, Miss Hamilton-King,' he said politely. 'I visited your home, Edenthorpe, once or twice when Billy and I managed to get leave together. You had a charming sister called Emily, I remember.'

'That's right. She's married now.'

'I'm not surprised. She was an extremely pretty young woman. But tell me—how did you manage to find me?'

'Your old regiment gave me your address in

Darlington. It was your mother who told us you were working here as a pianist.'

'Yes,' he said with a slight grimace of distaste as he looked around the seedy establishment, 'one has to make one's living the best one can these days. What with the strikes—and being handicapped the way I am—there was nothing for me in Darlington.' He sighed, taking a long drink of his whisky like a man who was used to it, and shaking his head slowly, a sadness causing his shoulders to droop.

'I lost a lot of friends in the War—brave and gallant men. But it was a bad job about poor Billy. I missed him, you know, when he didn't return to France. As a soldier, one expects to be killed fighting the enemy on the battlefield—not on the streets of home.' He suddenly gave Cordelia a puzzled look. 'Why did you want to find me? It must be important to bring you all the way from Leeds. It has to have something to do with Billy?'

'Yes, it has, although I don't live at Edenthorpe any more. I have a flat not far from here—in Bloomsbury, in fact, so it's within walking distance. If I had known you were so close, I would have come and seen you before now.'

'May I ask why?'

'I was hoping you could throw some light on Billy's death.'

'I doubt it. I'd just returned to France when I heard he'd been killed in an air raid on London.'

Taking a deep breath, Cordelia at last asked the question uppermost in her mind, looking at him directly. 'Did you know a woman by the name of Pamela Frankland, Mr Martin?'

He stared at her with something like shock registering in his eyes, suddenly appearing ill at ease, giving Cordelia the impression that this was a subject he would be reluctant to discuss.

'Pamela? Good Lord, yes—but look—really, I don't think that's—'

'You are right to think it's none of my business,' said Cordelia in sudden desperation, 'but in a way it is. Were you having an affair with her, Mr Martin? Please—you have to tell me.'

'Why? What has that to do with anything?'

'You do know she was killed in the same air raid on London that killed Billy?'

'Yes, I do.'

'And did you know that Billy's body was pulled from the rubble of the same hotel as Pamela's?'

Absolute astonishment registered in his eyes. 'Good Lord—no. Of course I didn't. What was he doing there?'

'I don't know. I was hoping you could tell me. You see, Captain Frankland, Pamela's husband, is of the opinion that Billy was having an affair with his wife—as were my parents when all the evidence was presented to them.'

'What? Billy and Pamela? That's ridiculous. If it weren't so tragic a matter, it would be laughable.

Billy was the epitome of everything that was right and good.'

'I know—but you have no idea how much everyone has suffered because of this, Mr Martin,' Cordelia said softly. 'Or of the anger and bitterness Captain Frankland feels for my family—which, on the evidence provided, is quite justified.

'Please correct me if I'm wrong, but I believe Billy has taken the blame for your own indiscretion. You cannot imagine the shame and humiliation my parents have suffered—as did the woman he was to have married. It is important that they—and Captain Frankland—are told the truth. I believe only you can do that.'

He was thoughtful for a moment before nodding slowly. 'Yes, you are right.'

He took another long drink of whisky, casting his mind back to that fateful day when Billy and Pamela had been killed. A weariness seemed to descend on him when memories began to penetrate his mind.

'I met Pamela on an earlier leave at a party in London. We were attracted to each other and began having an affair. That she had a husband fighting on the front didn't seem to matter to her—or to me, I'm ashamed to admit. One took one's happiness where one could in those days without a thought of the consequences, knowing when one returned to the War, where men were being blown to bits every hour of every day—like animals in an abattoir being led to the slaughter—there was every chance you would end up being one of them.'

His words were spoken slowly and with bitterness, as if it hurt to speak them. He seemed to look into the distance, the room and the people about him becoming nothing but mere shadows. His low, resonant voice went on with a sound almost of desolation.

'On the day of the air raid, Pamela and I met at the hotel where we always met when I was home on leave. Billy was travelling down from Leeds and had arranged to meet me there. We were to travel back to France together. When he didn't arrive, I assumed he must have been late getting to London and hadn't time to go to the hotel. So I left.

'It was not until I reached France that I heard about the air raid on London and Billy's and Pamela's deaths. But not for one moment did I realise Billy's name had been linked with that of Pamela's—or the grief this caused. I'm sorry. What else can I say?'

Cordelia sighed, sorry she had been forced to come here and make him aware that, through his actions, so much unhappiness had been caused.

'It would seem that Billy did go to the hotel, but not before you left. Pamela must still have been in bed.'

'Yes. It was ten o'clock at night when I left her.'

'At least we now know what he was doing there. I suspected all along that that was what happened but there was no way, without speaking to you, that I could prove this.'

'Do you know Captain Frankland?'

'Yes. I was employed as his secretary for a time.'

'And was he the strait-jacket Pamela described him as being?'

'No. Not at all. Captain Frankland is a fine man. What was Pamela like?'

'Oh,' he said, smiling slightly, a softness entering his eyes and his voice when he remembered the beautiful Pamela Frankland, 'she was beautiful—fun-loving—totally uninhibited with a free, erotic attitude and a wonderful zest for life. She hated the country. When her husband went off to France, she lived in London.

'Oh, I wasn't the first chap she'd had an affair with. She made no secret of that and it didn't seem to matter much to her. She used to throw wild parties—Greek parties, masquerades, Russian parties, you name it. Pamela knew how to enjoy herself.'

There was a remoteness in his eyes when he spoke of the woman who, for a brief period in his life, had enabled him to forget the horrors of war.

It was with a sinking heart that Cordelia listened to him acclaiming Pamela's disreputable attributes, suddenly feeling extremely sorry for Alex when she realised how his wife must have disgraced and humiliated him.

'Will you help me clear Billy's name, Mr Martin? I can't tell you how much it would mean to my family.'

He sighed deeply, meeting her gaze and nodding slowly. 'Yes. All right. Billy was my friend—my closest friend. I reckon I owe him that, at least.'

'Thank you.' Cordelia rose. 'I'll pass on what you have told me to Captain Frankland, if you don't mind.'

Michael looked up at her curiously. 'It seems strange that he should employ you if, as you say, he felt so bitter towards Billy.'

'He didn't know who I was when I first went to work for him. I was in America at the time of Billy's death and believed he had been killed in France. I only found out myself recently the true manner of his death. When Captain Frankland discovered who I was, we both agreed that my employment with him should be terminated.'

A tightening had come over Cordelia's features which caused Michael to look at her quizzically. 'And when he learns what really happened—will you go back and work for him?'

She shook her head, pain and a deep sadness entering her eyes, which told both Michael and Jeremy that there was more to her relationship with Captain Frankland than either of them had realised.

'No. It's too late for that now. Goodbye, Mr Martin. However unpleasant the circumstances are that have brought me here today, I'm glad to have met you. Billy and I were extremely close, so I shall be more than happy to see this unfortunate affair resolved.'

Michael watched them go, engulfed with a deep self-loathing, hating to think Billy's family had been forced to suffer the consequences of his own reckless and irresponsible behaviour.

Cordelia regretted the meal she and Jeremy ate at the Italian restaurant after they had left Michael Martin, for the following morning she was violently sick. Thinking it was something she had eaten that didn't agree with her, she thought no more of it. She was surprised to get a telephone call from Maxine, who was in London to visit friends and the National Gallery. They met for lunch at Lyon's restaurant in the Strand, which was busy with a full complement of customers.

They had a delightful lunch, with Maxine, looking as elegant and dignified as ever, telling Cordelia all about her visit to the National Gallery, how things were at Stanfield and other inconsequential matters until she finally fell silent and looked seriously across at Cordelia, a sadness entering her eyes.

'It's good to see you again, Cordelia. I think about you often. I'm so glad you agreed to meet me.'

'Why on earth shouldn't I?'

'Well,' she sighed, 'taking into account all that has happened, I wouldn't have blamed you if you'd refused.'

'I wouldn't do that, Maxine,' she smiled, all the old warmth she had felt for the older woman shining through. 'I'm glad you telephoned me.'

'You're looking well—if a little pale. No doubt it's the country air you're missing. Will you be going home for Christmas?'

'I don't think so. I may go for New Year. I'm going to work in America shortly, Maxine. It will be like making a new start.'

'Yes, I know. Alex told me. He—told me he'd seen you when he came to London. How did he seem to you?'

'Oh—he was polite and courteous—but inside he's still as unyielding and unforgiving as he was when I left Stanfield,' she answered, wondering what Maxine would say if she knew what had really happened between them.

'I know. I do wish this business over Pamela was resolved.'

'It is, Maxine. In fact, I have written Alex a letter explaining everything. Will you give it to him?' She produced an envelope addressed to Alex from her bag and handed it to her.

Maxine took it, looking extremely puzzled. 'But—but how, Cordelia? Did you manage to find Michael Martin?'

'Yes. He's working here in London—playing the piano in a nightclub in Soho.'

'And—and was he having an affair with Pamela?' she asked hesitantly.

'Yes. He had been for some considerable time, it seems. He gave me the impression that he may have been in love with her at the time. Billy had gone to the hotel to meet him. They were to travel back to France together after being home on leave. Unfortunately, Billy was late arriving and Michael, assuming he must have gone on ahead, left the hotel.'

'Leaving Pamela in bed, no doubt,' said Maxine with a bitterness peculiar to her.

'Yes, it seems like it.' She fell silent, taking a sip of her tea before looking uneasily at Maxine. 'Maxine—did—did Pamela make Alex very unhappy?' she asked tentatively.

She nodded, her eyes filling with pain. 'Yes. His life was made quite wretched by her affairs. Every time she took a new lover, he died a thousand deaths.'

'He must have loved her a great deal.'

'No. He never did love Pamela, Cordelia,' she said quietly, looking at her steadily. 'That's why she began taking lovers—to punish him, you see. She never did forgive him for not loving her.'

Cordelia stared at her. This was not what she had expected to hear. 'Then—then why did he marry her?'

'It was what their families wanted and they were well acquainted—but the marriage began to fail almost from the start. Pamela was an only child—rich—spoilt—beautiful—a woman of enormous vivacity, and never knowing what it was like not to have what she wanted—and she wanted Alex to flaunt like one of her useless possessions. She never was a compliant wife.'

'Then why did they not divorce?'

'Because Alex refused to consider it.'

'But why—if he didn't love her?'

'My dear Cordelia—the Franklands were old-fashioned—their ways and traditions steeped in the last century. Family and honour meant everything to them. It was instilled into Alex from an early age. Divorce was quite out of the question then. But there were so many rows and recriminations that life became almost unbearable at Stanfield.'

'Then surely under those circumstances divorce would have been the best thing?'

'Yes, I think so too. But I did not interfere. During the war, when Alex was in France and the house had been turned into a convalescent hospital, Pamela spent all her time in London. Every time she took a new lover she made sure Alex knew about it.

'Unable to accept the situation any longer—or to withstand the disgrace she was determined to inflict on him—having reached the limits of his endurance, he relented and told her she could have a divorce. Unfortunately, she was killed before this could be implemented. The sordidness of the whole affair almost destroyed Alex.'

'I had no idea.'

'No, I know. Perhaps now you will understand why there are no photographs of her at Stanfield. Alex wanted nothing left around to remind him of her.'

At last Cordelia could understand the implacable hatred Alex felt for Billy. In his eyes, her brother had become all Pamela's faceless lovers rolled into one. Perhaps when he read her letter some of his bitterness would be eased. How she hoped so. Maxine had certainly given her something to think about.

But other things were beginning to occupy her mind. Her sickness in the mornings was becoming a regular occurrence, which made her change her mind and decide to go to Edenthorpe for Christmas after all. She telephoned her parents and told them to expect her.

By the time she went home three weeks later, almost all her mornings were the same, which left her feeling quite ill. It was only after a visit to the doctor that he confirmed a suspicion she hardly dared believe—that she was going to have Alex's child.

She was quite overwhelmed by her condition and it gave her a strange, agonising joy. Whatever happened now or in the future, Alex was bound to her by flesh and blood. His child was the greatest gift he could have given her—and that it had been conceived during that one wonderful night they had spent in each other's arms filled her with exultation.

She was in no doubt that there would be battles to fight, for she was well aware of the terrible stigma attached to the word illegitimate. But she was determined to face any problems head-on in defence of this wonderful being growing inside her.

It was these thoughts that sustained her on the train taking her up to Leeds. The hardest thing of all would be telling her parents, but she wouldn't tell them just yet. She wanted to keep her secret for the time being, to nurse it and cherish it, until the time came when she could no longer hide it.

One thing she would have to tell them—although she would put it off until after the New Year—was that she could not go to America—at least, not until after the baby was born. It would be like putting her career on hold until then. She was sure the Merlins wouldn't mind and, if the business was expanding, there would always be a vacancy for her.

In the letter she had written to Alex, the one she had given to Maxine, she wrote of her meeting with Michael Martin and that he had confirmed what she had suspected all along about Billy being at the hotel to meet him—and for no other reason. She gave him all the details of that meeting, and where Mr Martin could be contacted, should he wish to confirm what she wrote.

She told him nothing of the child, for the last thing she wanted was to blackmail him into coming to her because it was the right and decent thing to do. She wanted him to come to her because he loved her and for no other reason.

Chapter Thirteen

To the north of Leeds the Yorkshire moors in winter are beautiful in their desolation. It is a wild, featureless landscape, solitary and saddening, the shadows of light mist and dark blue and grey tints on the distant horizon forever changing—never the same when one looks at them twice. The only sounds to break the peace and tranquillity were the cry of a curlew and the gentle tumble of water in rocky streams.

Today the weather was cold, purifying the air. The ground was hard, and the occasional tree which had dared to grow, defying all the elements stood petrified, covered in a white hoar frost.

Walking off the excesses of goose, plum pudding and all the exotic delicacies one associates with Christmas, with Emily and her husband, Georgina and her two children and three energetic young terriers, Cordelia walked along the familiar paths, as she had done on countless occasions since childhood, towards their favourite destination—the waterfall, which cascaded over the shiny, ice-covered rocks from the moors up above.

They paused on the narrow stone bridge to indulge in a pastime which they so enjoyed in their own childhood: letting the children throw twigs off one side of the bridge into the crystal-clear water below, and run to the other side in glee and excited anticipation to see whose would be the first to come floating through. Often the twigs became stuck between the rocks under the bridge and the whole performance had to be enacted again.

It had been a lovely Christmas, with the family enjoying the occasion of being together once more, the only sadness being Billy's absence—although the atmosphere which had prevailed since his death, as Cordelia's parents had striven to keep the true nature of it from her, was lightened now it had been proved there had been nothing dishonourable or scandalous about it.

It was a happy group that returned to the house, going to find their parents in the drawing-room, which immediately became a cacophony of noise from children and dogs alike.

Cordelia followed them inside, her cheeks flushed from her walk, her eyes shining brightly and her lips parted in a broad smile as she laughed at something funny Emily's husband had just said to her—until she became aware of the still figure sitting in a chair, who rose when he saw her, his eyes meeting hers, and her heart leaped.

Thrown off balance, she stared at him uncomprehendingly. Immediately the smile froze on her lips, although her heart was overflowing with gladness, and it was all she could do to stop herself from casting herself into his arms. There was a silence in the room as everyone else became aware of the presence of this terribly handsome, if somewhat aloof, gentleman.

Polite introductions were made, after which Georgina and Emily ushered the protesting children and dogs out of the room, leaving Alex and Cordelia alone with her parents, who were noticeably quiet. They moved towards their daughter, having been surprised by Captain Frankland's unexpected arrival at Edenthorpe, and yet happy he had come and the whole unfortunate business concerning Billy's death had been resolved.

'We'll leave you alone with Captain Frankland, Cordelia. I'm sure you have much to talk about,' said her mother, turning once more to their visitor. 'You'll stay to dinner, Captain Frankland, won't you?'

'Thank you, Lady Langhorne, but no—I'm afraid I shall have to get back to Doncaster.'

A look of disappointment crossed her face, for she liked this good-looking stranger, and would be more than happy for Cordelia to resume her work at Stanfield Hall—where there was every chance they would become close—instead of her going off to America to work in some art gallery. 'Well—perhaps some other time, then?'

'Yes. I'd like that.'

When they were alone at last, Alex moved towards Cordelia, who had not altered her position since entering the room. He was smiling suavely, as though it was the most natural thing in the world that he should be there. But, whatever it was that had brought him to Edenthorpe, she was glad to see him. Although greeting him now, with a proper degree of casualness, was more difficult than she had expected when she remembered their last encounter.

'Hello, Cordelia,' he said softly, realising how much he had missed her. It was the first time he had seen her so apparently carefree and casual and he thought how much it suited her. How lovely and vibrant she looked, with her hair all mussed up and her skin aglow from her walk on the moors. At that moment he wanted nothing else in the world but to make love to her.

Maxine had told him she was to remain in London for Christmas, so he had not been prepared to see her here at Edenthorpe. When he had received her letter, he had been plagued with so many conflicting emotions where she and her family were concerned, becoming lost in a turmoil of contradiction and insoluble dilemma. It was only right that he saw her parents, to express his sincere apologies and regrets over the awful injustice that had been done to their son.

If Cordelia's mind was still set on going to America, then he considered it in both their best interests not to see each other again. That was why he had chosen now to come to Edenthorpe—and also the fact that he did not trust himself to see her, for it would surely shatter his every vestige of reason and resistance. When her mother had told him she had decided to come home for Christmas after all, he had not been prepared for the surge of gladness that had almost unmanned him.

'Alex! What on earth are you doing here?'

'When I got your letter explaining everything, I thought that the least I could do was to come and see your parents. I was in the north anyway—staying with friends in Doncaster, so I wasn't too far away.'

'I see. Are you buying more horses?'

'Merely looking, at present. Your parents and I have discussed the matter which brings me here and we all realise that a terrible, yet understandable, mistake has been made.'

'Did you go and see Michael Martin to confirm what I told you?'

'No. I had no wish to have any contact with one of my wife's old lovers,' he said with deep bitterness. 'I took your word for what happened.'

'Then it's a pity you did not listen to me earlier. I had every faith in my brother, Alex. I knew he would never have done anything so dishonourable.'

'Forgive me, Cordelia,' he said dryly, 'but, unfortunately, I did not know your brother so I acted on the evidence given to me.'

'Yes, of course,' she replied stiffly. 'I'm just glad it's all over and done with and Billy can be mourned with the respect he deserved.'

'Maxine told me you were staying in London for Christmas.'

She glanced at him sharply, experiencing a strong rush of disappointment. 'So—you didn't expect to find me here. Is that why you came at this time? To avoid seeing me?'

'Of course not,' Alex answered, although he was not being entirely truthful. 'It's good to see you again. You know that.'

'Do I?' she asked pointedly. She wanted to ask him why he had not telephoned her or written. Didn't he realise how bewildered and upset she would be by his sudden departure that morning, after they had spent such a wonderful, unforgettable night together—without even a tender word of goodbye?

'You should,' he said quietly.

Cordelia sighed, facing him, uncertain suddenly. Once again she felt that the invisible wall, which had been between them in the early days of their relationship, had re-erected itself, and she felt a terrible wrench inside.

'I did intend staying in London—but there wasn't much happening so I changed my mind,' she said, moving away from him, averting her gaze, for she found his nearness disconcerting. His close scrutiny of her features was making her feel suddenly uncomfortable, as though it might provide an answer to some question he had in mind. 'Besides, because I am off to America shortly, I wanted to spend as much time with my family as possible before I go.'

'You are still going to New York?' he asked quietly, still looking at her in a peculiar way—as though she might be hiding something.

'Yes,' she whispered, knowing as she said this that she was lying. She felt, rather than knew, that Alex was looking at her, for she could almost feel his eyes boring into her. 'It's too good an offer to turn down,' she said quietly, at last turning to look at him, the distance he insisted on keeping between them almost bringing tears to her eyes, tears she was too proud and too angry to shed.

She had a wild desire to hold out her arms to him, to beg him to ask her not to go, but she couldn't. Oh, why didn't he give her the opportunity to tell him how she felt—and that she was going to have his child? And why did he continue his close scrutiny of her features, which was making her feel uncomfortable, as though it might provide an answer to some question he had in mind?

If only Cordelia knew how desperately Alex wanted to get down on his knees and declare his love for her all over again, to ask her to become his wife and return with him to Stanfield. But he couldn't. She had clearly made up her mind about going to New York and she was right. It was too good an opportunity for her to turn down. It wouldn't be fair of him to try and dissuade her.

'Yes, you're right. I'm sure you'll get on well in America. No one is more aware of your complete dedication to your work then I am myself. I am sure you will do well for yourself and meet with every success in your new venture. You deserve it, Cordelia.'

'Thank you,' she answered with great difficulty, sensing he was about to leave her and determined she wasn't going to cry. She was on the point of confessing how much she loved him, but recollected herself. She tried to smile, but her lips trembled.

She took a deep breath, hoping to put some conviction into her words. 'I'm looking forward to it. A new challenge is just what I need right now. I learnt a lot about the world of art from you, Alex. Hopefully it will come in useful.'

'Yes, I'm sure it will.' He stepped back, a wintry smile touching his lips. 'Goodbye, Cordelia—and good luck.'

'Thank you, Alex,' she whispered.

She stared at him before he turned away from her, looking for some sign of weakness that would tell her he still loved her, but his face was expressionless, and his grey eyes, having lost all their warmth, were like ice. He seemed to have become a man of iron. She was unable to believe that he was going to dismiss her so lightly from his life. Did she mean nothing to him after all?

He turned swiftly from her and walked to the door. Cordelia did not move but it took nearly all her willpower to prevent herself from crying out, begging him not to leave her.

In his turn Alex also suffered, and as he went out into the hall to bid farewell to her parents, she did not see the move he made to the closed door to go back to her, or the pain in his eyes when he again turned away, believing it was useless.

If only each had been aware of the other's thoughts, Alex would not have left her then.

It was with a heavy heart that Cordelia returned to London, in a quandary as to what to do next. She couldn't go to America until after her child was born, and Edenthorpe was out of the question because her morning sickness continued to plague her. Eventually, her mother was bound to suspect there was something wrong and she wasn't ready to tell anyone just yet.

She resigned herself to remaining at the flat,

although it would seem empty, for Kitty had arranged to spend some time with her family before going on holiday. She would be gone five weeks. She even contemplated taking a holiday herself, somewhere warm—France or Italy, perhaps—but decided against it in the end.

Kitty was deeply concerned about Cordelia and had been convinced for some time now that something was terribly wrong. She had certainly not been herself ever since she had returned to London after spending Christmas at Edenthorpe.

There was a strained look on her pale face. She was constantly on edge and had taken to going out for long walks, which, Kitty suspected, was in order to avoid telling her what was really troubling her. It wasn't like her. Having become as close as sisters over the years they had known each other, normally they confided in each other when something was wrong, but now, whenever Cordelia met Kitty's questioning eyes, she became awkward and evasive.

It was Cordelia's early-morning discomfort that finally told her what was wrong. After a particularly bad bout of sickness one morning Kitty confronted her, going in to Cordelia's room where she lay curled miserably up on the bed, her head buried in the pillows.

'How are you feeling, Cordelia?' she asked, her voice soft with concern.

Cordelia averted her eyes, immediately on the

defensive. 'A bit sick, that's all. I must have eaten something that doesn't agree with me.'

Kitty sat beside her on the bed, frowning with apprehension. 'We both know that isn't the reason. You're like this most mornings—I know—I've heard you.'

She sighed deeply. 'This isn't like you, Cordelia. I thought we always told each other everything. There's never been any constraint between us and we've always been honest with each other. You're pregnant, aren't you?' she said gently. 'How long did you think you could go on trying to hide it from me?'

For a moment there was silence and then very slowly Cordelia sat up and looked her friend straight in the eye, her expression one of anguish.

'Yes, Kitty,' she admitted softly, 'I am pregnant. Unquestionably so. I wanted to tell you, but—'

Noting the catch in her voice and the sudden tears awash in her eyes, Kitty reached out and grasped her hand, silencing her. 'Don't, Cordelia. Don't upset yourself. It doesn't matter.'

'But it does.'

'Alex Frankland is the father, isn't he?'

Cordelia nodded miserably. 'Who else? Oh, Kitty, I've been such a fool. I should never have let it happen.'

'We're all entitled to make mistakes, love. Even you.'

'But I thought he loved me, Kitty. I thought

when he went to Edenthorpe he wanted to see me—but it was my parents he wanted to see, to express his regrets over Billy. He thought I was staying in London for Christmas, otherwise he wouldn't have gone.'

'Have you told your parents about the baby?'

She shook her head. 'No, not yet. No one knows—just you. They're going to be so terribly disappointed in me when I tell them.'

'What about Alex? When will you tell him?'

Cordelia lowered her eyes and shook her head, tears slowly spilling over her lashes and running unheeded down her cheeks. Kitty stared at her when she suddenly realised that she had no intention of telling him.

'You are going to tell him, Cordelia? You have to.'

'No. I can't. I don't want him to know. I love him, Kitty. I never thought I would love anyone as much as I do Alex. But I can't tell him. I want him to come to me because he loves me—not to do the decent thing by me for the sake of the child.'

'But don't you think he has a right to know?'

'Perhaps. But he knew what he was doing that night, and not once afterwards did he contact me to see if I was all right.'

Kitty sighed, deeply affected by Cordelia's predicament. 'I do so wish I hadn't told my parents I would visit them. I can't leave you like this.'

Cordelia wiped her tear-streaked face with her hands as she tried to pull herself together. 'Of course you must. It's ages since you went home. You mustn't disappoint them on account of me.'

'No, Cordelia. I don't like the idea of you being here in the flat alone. I'm sure they won't mind and I can easily cancel my holiday.'

Cordelia smiled at her gratefully. 'Bless you, Kitty, but no. You must go. I'll be fine, really. Besides—it will give me an opportunity to think seriously about what I am going to do—about the baby and my career.'

Kitty was about to insist but on seeing the level, determined expression in Cordelia's eyes she sighed resignedly. 'Well—if you're sure you'll be all right.'

'Of course I will. Don't worry about me and go and enjoy your holiday—but what I've told you is between us for the time being, Kitty. There's no need for anyone to know until I've made some decisions about the future.'

Kitty smiled and squeezed her hand. 'Don't worry. Your secret is safe with me.'

The flat seemed strangely quiet when Kitty had left. At first Cordelia took pleasure in being alone, but after a few days the solitude began to get on her nerves. She worried ceaselessly about her problems, anxiously seeking solutions, but none came. She thought constantly about Alex, unable to banish him from her thoughts, taking long walks through the streets of London in an attempt to clear him from her mind but it was impossible.

It was almost a week after Kitty's departure that she opened the door and saw Alex standing there, tall and proud, his black hair slightly ruffled from the wind howling outside.

Cordelia stared at him, unable to read his expression or his feelings. All she was aware of was that he was here—he had come to her. He stood looking down at her with his wonderful grey eyes and everything, except the glow of love she carried for him, was swept away, for that was all that mattered just then. After a brief silence Alex was the first to speak.

'Aren't you going to ask me in?'

'Oh, yes, yes—of course,' she replied, suddenly nervous, having just got out of the bath and conscious that her hair was wet and she was only wearing a bathrobe.

Alex stepped inside and she closed the door behind him. His eyes studied her carefully, admiringly. Cordelia felt a marvellous elation waking inside her. She looked at him, loving him—wanting him.

'What are you doing here, Alex?'

'I think you know the answer to that,' he said quietly. 'You don't mind, do you?'

'You know I don't.'

'Good. So you're not going to send me away?'

'How could I? I'm flattered that you've come to see me at all. Please—take off your coat and come and sit down. I apologise for greeting you dressed like this, but I've just got out of the bath.'

'Don't apologise,' he smiled, his eyes raking her body from head to foot appraisingly. 'You look divine.' He removed his coat and hung it on a stand behind the door. 'Where is your friend? Is she not at home?'

'No. Kitty's gone to stay with her parents for a while.'

'I see.' He smiled, quietly delighted, thinking that he couldn't have chosen a more appropriate time to come and see her. 'How long will she be away?'

'A-about five weeks.'

He nodded, unsmiling now, digesting this seriously. He moved away from her towards the window and stood looking out, his hands clasped behind his back. The light was beginning to fade as he gazed out at the buildings and lights of London.

Cordelia went and stood beside him, wet tendrils of her hair encapsulating her exquisite face. Alex turned and looked down at her, smelling the delicate perfume of her body, seeing how calm and smooth her skin was, and how her parted lips were soft and vulnerable. His grey eyes became serious, caressing her face.

'I've missed you, Cordelia.'

'Have you? I've missed you, too,' she admitted, meeting his gaze.

'After I left Edenthorpe I went through hell. I couldn't bear the thought of you going to New York without knowing how I felt. I had to see you, although I wondered if I might be too late. You cannot imagine the absolute relief I felt when you opened the door.'

He reached out and turned aside a stray tendril of her hair that was close to her eyes, which were wide open and clear. 'I had to tell you that I love you. To ask you to become my wife. I realised when I returned to Stanfield that you were all that mattered to me. I could not live the rest of my life away from you. Even if the matter concerning your brother had not been resolved, I believe I would have come here.'

'Then why didn't you tell me at Edenthorpe?'

'Because I knew how important your career was to you. You seemed so sure, so determined that that was what you wanted. I did not wish to complicate matters for you.'

Cordelia stared at him, realising at last that his indifference had been a pose, that all the time his need, his love for her, had been as great as her own was for him.

'Oh, Alex—why didn't you tell me? You were right. My career was important to me—it still is, but it is not as important as what I feel for you. You must have known how I felt,' she said softly.

'You must have known how much I loved you that night we spent together. Do you think I could give myself to any man—as I did to you that night—whom I did not love? Can you imagine how I felt when I awoke and found you gone? I waited for you to come to me—to telephone—to write—anything, and when there was nothing I believed I had meant nothing to you after all.'

Struck by the awareness of the despair and physical suffering he had put her through since that night, Alex gathered her into his arms, drawing her slender, trembling body close to his hard chest, placing his lips on her hair.

'You're the most important, the most precious person in the world to me. What a fool I've been,' he murmured. 'After the way I've behaved, I deserved to lose you.' His arms tightened about her and she lifted her face to his, dazzled by this moment of joy.

'I cannot believe this is happening,' she whispered. 'I keep imagining it is all a dream and that soon I shall wake up. After all that has happened, I cannot believe you love me.'

He smiled, placing his lips against her own. 'Do I really have to show you?' he murmured.

'Yes,' she said, sliding her arms tenderly round his neck and drawing his face down to her. 'I think you do.'

* * *

That night they were alone on an island of rapture, where they could forget all about the real world. Their love-making reached an intensity neither of them had experienced before. It was torture and delight.

They were besotted with each other, taking pleasure from each other—their touch, their lips—warm and demanding of each other, which sent senses soaring higher and higher as they reached the peak of their love-making, granting each other fulfilment before sighing and sleeping, wrapped in a sweet delirium of unimaginable bliss.

It was as the sun was rising the next morning that Alex found Cordelia absent from the bed. He heard her in the bathroom—she sounded ill, as if she were being sick. And then he knew. It came to him in a blinding flash what was wrong with her. He was up when she came back into the bedroom. At the sight of her ashen face, he folded her in his arms.

'You little fool,' he admonished gently, kissing the top of her head. 'Why didn't you tell me? You are pregnant, aren't you, Cordelia?'

She nodded, feeling terrible. Yes.'

'Don't you think you should have told me?'

'You've no idea how much I wanted to, but I couldn't,' she said miserably, continuing to let him hold her. 'I wanted *you*, Alex. I didn't want you to marry me because of the child. I wanted you to want me. Don't you understand?'

Alex stared down at her, his face expressing bewilderment, disbelief and finally agony as the realisation of what she had intended dawned on him. After what seemed like a lifetime later, he held her away from him, forcing her to look at him, his grey eyes hard and intense.

'When were you going to tell me, Cordelia? When?'

He was holding her shoulders, his grip so powerful it hurt. His eyes stared hard into hers, demanding an answer. Cordelia shook her head, turning her face away, feeling so dreadfully sick, and in her weakened state she didn't want to fight. He took her chin in his fingers and forced her to face him, her eyes full of a mournful sadness.

'Look at me, Cordelia. Come—don't lie to me. You were going to tell me, weren't you? Assuming I am the father, of course.'

Cordelia stared at him, hot, defenceless tears welling up in her eyes at his anger. 'Of course you are. There has never been anyone else.'

'Then what did you intend by keeping such an important matter from me? Was it some kind of test you were putting me through? A test of my love?'

He shook his head slowly, in disbelief and disappointment when she didn't answer.

'Oh, Cordelia—I think you take your independence too far. What if I hadn't come here to see you? What would you have done? Would you have let me live my life ignorant of the fact that I had a child somewhere?'

When she refused to answer, in his outrage Alex flung himself away from her, unable to believe she would have done anything as cruel as that, and then with a calm, businesslike manner, he began to dress, and only then did he speak to her again, looking down at her where she was crying softly, face down into a pillow.

Patiently he said, 'I'm going out, Cordelia.'

Slowly she turned her tear-streaked face up to him, seeing the pain still raw in his eyes. 'Out? But where are you going?'

'You'll find out when I return. You must understand that I had a right to know about this. From now on we shall make any decisions regarding our child together. Is that clear, Cordelia?'

He turned then and left her.

When Alex returned many hours later Cordelia was waiting for him. Her face was pale and tense—evidence of the nervous strain she had been under since his departure. She had no idea where he had gone or if he would return. She only knew that she had never felt so miserable before in her life. She had been foolish to keep any knowledge of the child from him, she knew that now. But he had to come back and forgive her. She asked for nothing else.

He did come back, with the most wonderful

bouquet of flowers. They filled her arms and far from being angry now, he kissed her lips as though nothing untoward had happened between them. She stared at him in amazement.

'Alex—what is this? Where have you been?'

'I have been arranging our wedding, my love.'

Cordelia's eyes opened wide in astonishment. 'Wedding?'

He smiled down at her. 'We are getting married next week. Is that time enough for you to prepare yourself?'

Cordelia flung herself into his arms, not knowing whether to laugh or cry with happiness. 'Thank you,' she whispered. 'You don't know how happy that makes me.' She leaned back in his arms and looked at him. 'Please forgive me, Alex. I have been very stupid—I know that now.'

'Yes, you have,' he said gravely, 'but we'll say no more about that—so long as you promise me you will never do anything so foolish again. There must always be trust between us, Cordelia. After the terrible years I spent being married to Pamela—who purposely set out to humiliate me at every opportunity because I did not love her—it is important to me.'

Looking into his eyes, Cordelia was overwhelmed with love and understanding. 'Yes—I know. And I do promise, Alex.'

'Then that is settled,' he murmured, folding her in his arms once more. 'Our wedding will just be a civil ceremony—no grand society affair, which I'm sure will disappoint your mother. Will your parents mind if we don't get married at Edenthorpe?'

'No—at least, not my father. All he has ever wanted is my happiness. And mother—as you say, she will be disappointed to have missed out on another big society wedding in the family, but when she's got over the initial shock, then I know she will be more than happy that I'm getting married at all. I think she'd given up on me.'

'Do you want them to come down for the wedding.'

She shook her head. 'No. I want it to be as quiet as possible—just the two of us—and the baby, of course,' she smiled. 'I don't want anything to spoil it. I'll tell my parents afterwards—and about the baby.'

'Will you mind giving up your career to become Lady Frankland?'

'No,' and she smiled impishly. 'Although I might apply for the position of your secretary again—or I might even go one better and apply to be your estate agent. Would you consider your wife for the position, do you think?'

'My darling Cordelia, once this child of ours is born you can be anything you want to be. Will I have any say in the matter?'

'No,' she murmured, her lips close to his. 'But

the position I am looking forward to most of all is that of being your wife.'

After Cordelia and Alex were married in a quiet, civil ceremony, they took advantage of Kitty's absence and remained in the flat for a further three weeks—weeks made up of long days, filled with simple, joyous pleasures. They enjoyed London in a carefree way as Cordelia had done when she had been plain Miss King.

They ate at wonderful restaurants, spent long hours wandering through the parks and down by the river, indifferent to the fact that the weather was cold, before strolling back to the flat—often the silvery light of the moon guiding their way. There they would fall into bed and make love, and sometimes, wrapped in each other's arms, they would discuss the future and the baby, and these were the times when Cordelia realised her reason for living.

When she lay in Alex's arms, she prayed that their lives together would be as fulfilling and wonderful as these weeks had been—and the first part of her prayer was granted when their son was born at Stanfield Hall.

Historical Romance™

Coming next month

LETTERS TO A LADY

Gail Whitiker

Devon Royce, Earl of Marwood, was content. Napoleon was on the run and Devon had finally found the woman of his dreams. But when he caught Charlotte, his betrothed, embracing a stranger, he did what any right-thinking man would do—he broke off the betrothal. After all, his honour was at stake.

Nevertheless, for the sake of appearances, he agreed to Charlotte's scheme to keep the news a secret—for now. But Devon was uncomfortable with the false betrothal. He wanted a chance to woo Charlotte all over again. Maybe this time they could get it right!

LADY CLAIRVAL'S MARRIAGE

Paula Marshall

On returning from a stay in the country, Luke Harcourt found his landlady had taken in a new lodger. Mrs Anne Cowper was apparently a sempstress, and was a very quiet and withdrawn lady, who intrigued Luke when she showed flashes of wit and humour. Despite the efforts of his landlady to keep them apart, Luke and Anne became close friends, and she even allowed him to escort her to Islington Fair. But that fun-filled, pleasurable day had consequences neither could have foreseen, which sent them fleeing through the countryside to Haven's End—where only fiery strength and determination could win Luke the lady he loved...

Return this coupon and we'll send you 4 Historical Romance novels and a mystery gift absolutely FREE! We'll even pay the postage and packing for you.

We're making you this offer to introduce you to the benefits of the Reader Service™– FREE home delivery of brand-new Historical Romance novels, at least a month before they are available in the shops, FREE gifts and a monthly Newsletter packed with information, competitions, author profiles and lots more...

Accepting these FREE books and gift places you under no obligation to buy, you may cancel at any time, even after receiving just your free shipment. Simply complete the coupon below and send it to:

MILLS & BOON READER SERVICE, FREEPOST, CROYDON, SURREY, CR9 3WZ.

READERS IN EIRE PLEASE SEND COUPON TO PO BOX 4546, DUBLIN 24

NO STAMP NEEDED

Yes, please send me 4 free Historical Romance novels and a mystery gift. I understand that unless you hear from me, I will receive 4 superb new titles every month for just £2.99* each, postage and packing free. I am under no obligation to purchase any books and I may cancel or suspend my subscription at any time, but the free books and gift will be mine to keep in any case. (I am over 18 years of age)

H7XE

Ms/Mrs/Miss/Mr ______________________________

BLOCK CAPS PLEASE

Address ______________________________

____

______________ Postcode ______________

mps MAILING PREFERENCE SERVICE

Offer closes 30th September 1997. We reserve the right to refuse an application. *Prices and terms subject to change without notice. Offer only valid in UK and Ireland and is not available to current subscribers to this series. Overseas readers please write for details.

DMA

You may be mailed with offers from other reputable companies as a result of this application. Please tick box if you would prefer not to receive such offers. ☐